YULE BE MY DUKE

MATCHMAKING CHRONICLES
BOOK ONE

DARCY BURKE

Zealous Quill Press

Yule Be My Duke
Copyright © 2023 Darcy Burke
All rights reserved.
ISBN: 9781637261781

Book design: © Darcy Burke.
Book Cover Design: © Dar Albert, Wicked Smart Designs.
Editing: Lindsey Faber.

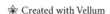 Created with Vellum

YULE BE MY DUKE

The Matchmaking Chronicles

The course of true love never runs smooth. Sometimes a little matchmaking is required. When couples meet at a house party, what could go wrong?

It was loathe at first sight when Cecilia Bromwell met John Rowley, the Earl of Cosford five years ago at a party where his ill-conceived prank and irascible temper ruined not one but two of her new gowns. Now, at a Yuletide house party, Cecilia learns their parents seek to match them in wedded bliss. However, she has no interest in even speaking with the "Menace," especially after he spills wine down her bodice, ruining yet *another* gown.

John has no desire to be paired with the "Shrew" for the Yule log hunt. But if they can suffer each other's company for a short time, perhaps they can convince their parents that they do *not* suit. When they're separated from everyone else and a snowstorm drives them to seek shelter alone in a cottage together, it may not matter what they want.

With marriage all but imminent, can these enemies become lovers by morning?

Don't miss the rest of the *Matchmaking Chronicles*!

Do you want to hear all the latest about me and my books? Sign up at Reader Club newsletter for members-only bonus content, advance notice of pre-orders, insider scoop, as well as contests and giveaways!

Care to share your love for my books with like-minded readers? Want to hang with me and see pictures of my cats (who doesn't!)? Then don't miss my exclusive Facebook groups!

Darcy's Duchesses for historical readers
Burke's Book Lovers for contemporary readers

Want more historical romance? Do you like your historical romance filled with passion and red hot chemistry? Join me and my author friends in the Facebook group, Historical Harlots, for exclusive giveaways, chat with amazing HistRom authors, and more!

CHAPTER 1

December 1786

Cecilia Bromwell had visited Broadheath on several occasions, but only once before in the presence of a certain gentleman. Not that he'd been a gentleman five years ago—he'd been a horrid, arrogant, rude scoundrel. She expected he would be precisely the same now.

"You're certain he'll be here?" she asked Dinah Gladwin, the Baroness Spetchley. Of average height with chestnut-brown hair and moss-green eyes, Dinah was a white woman the same age as Cecilia.

Dinah was a long-time friend. Indeed, she'd been here on that occasion five years ago, another house party but in the summer, when John Rowley, the Earl of Cosford had been so hideously awful. Awful enough that she'd called him the Menace, and now it was the only way she could think of him.

"Yes, I'm certain," Dinah said rather breathlessly. "I *saw* the Menace earlier."

"Blast!" Cecilia flounced onto a chair in her bedchamber where Dinah had come to see her. "Why didn't my parents inform me?" She was certain her mother would remember how horribly the Menace had treated her.

"Perhaps they didn't know?"

"I would be surprised if my mother wasn't well aware of the entire guest list. She makes it her business to know who will be anywhere, especially a party like this." How else could she make matches, which the women in her family had been doing for centuries?

Dinah pursed her lips. "She definitely knew. And she didn't tell you. What does that mean?"

"I don't know, but I have a terribly anxious feeling."

Gasping, Dinah sank onto the other chair. "You don't think she wants to…match the two of you?"

"I bloody well hope not." Except her mother and father had been disappointed when she hadn't wed last Season. At twenty, she was more than old enough. She had to consider that was her mother's intent—to see her betrothed before the end of the party. But to *the Menace*? "Whom else did you see here?"

"Only Sophia and Priest." She referred to their friend Sophia, who'd also been at that party five years ago, and her new husband, Michael Priestly.

"Another married couple like you and Spetch," Cecilia observed. "If there are no other young unmarrieds here, I am *doomed*."

"They can't make you marry him," Dinah said with fiery defiance, her green eyes sparking.

Cecilia folded her arms over her chest and frowned. "They will try very, very hard. I'd rather marry a snake."

"Oh!" Dinah laughed. "Of course a snake."

Because the Menace had put a snake in the boat Cecilia and Dinah had been in on the lake five years ago. Dinah had shrieked in terror as she'd stood up. Her movement had capsized the craft, and they'd had to be rescued. "I can't believe Spetch remains friendly with him, particularly after he married you." Cecilia clucked her tongue.

"Spetch thought it was an amusing prank, until we fell into the water. But he didn't hold a grudge against Cosford. You can't expect him—or me—to be angry with him for something that happened five years ago." Dinah rushed to add, "However, I completely understand why you hold him in poor esteem."

"No, I don't expect that of you or Spetch," Cecilia said with a sigh, dropping her hands to her sides.

Dinah stood. "Come, let's go downstairs. Aren't you even the slightest bit curious to see Cosford after all this time?"

Cecilia looked up at her. "No." She brushed at her skirt. "You go ahead."

"All right." Dinah hesitated. "Don't let him ruin your fun. It will be a wonderful party. You'll see."

Only if Cecilia managed to stay away from her nemesis.

As Dinah left, Cecilia's mother came in. Her blonde hair was immaculately styled as usual, and she was garbed in the height of fashion, a rich blue velvet gown with gold bows adorning the bodice. Pearls adorned her neck and swung from her ears. She said a few words to Dinah before closing the door and coming toward Cecilia. "Don't you want to go downstairs with Dinah?"

"Not yet." Cecilia stood. She meant to hold her temper, truly, but she just knew her mother was scheming. "With whom are you planning to match me at this party?"

Her mother's mouth stretched into a tight but brief smile. "Shall we sit?"

"No." Cecilia crossed her arms again. "It better not be the Me—Cosford."

Her mother's eyes flickered with surprise. "Why not?"

"You know how I detest him, how awful he is."

"Actually, no, I didn't realize you detest him. He's not awful. He's an earl and heir to a dukedom."

"His titles don't make him palatable. He's a menace." Cecilia lowered her arms and fisted her hands at her sides. "How can you not know how much I loathe him? Have you forgotten what he did to me five years ago at this very estate?"

The baroness frowned and looked beyond Cecilia, as if she could see into the past. "I suppose I have. What did he do?"

Cecilia groaned. "He put that snake in my boat, and we capsized. He ruined my new green-and-pink dress. You were furious."

"I vaguely remember that," her mother murmured.

"And then he poured lemonade over my head, ruining my new butter-yellow dress—the one with the embroidered flowers."

"Oh! That *did* make me angry," the baroness said with a slight pout. She shook her head and focused on Cecilia. "Well, that was five years ago, and we must hope his manner has improved."

Hope? "Or you can find someone else to match me with," Cecilia said with an overabundance of sweetness so that her mother narrowed one eye at her.

"You haven't wanted any of the others I've proposed."

"Because I couldn't love them. You know how I feel about falling in love. It's absolutely necessary. I couldn't possibly love Cosford." Cecilia shuddered at the thought. He was utterly deplorable.

Her mother exhaled, sounding beleaguered. She took Cecilia's hand. "I know love is important to you, and I've explained that to your father. He is less…concerned with that aspect. However, if you find Cosford intolerable, I will find someone else. But you must at least give him a chance."

"Cosford is aware of this potential match?" It turned Cecilia's stomach to even think those words: *potential match*, just as much as it nauseated her to call him by name. She much preferred the name he deserved: the Menace.

"I don't think so. Promise me that you will delay your judgment until after you spend some time with him—and you must be fair."

It didn't take Cecilia long at all to determine if she and a gentleman might suit. So far, only one had passed the initial meeting, and after a handful of encounters, she'd deduced there would never be any passion between them.

"I will *try*." Cecilia had no intention of doing so. She would tolerate the Menace for a day or two, then inform her mother that his insufferability had not diminished. Indeed, she imagined it had only swelled over the past five years. She might even need to revise his name to the Insufferable Menace.

"That is all I ask," her mother said, sounding a bit weary. "Now, let us go downstairs. I see you've changed since our arrival. You look fresh and lovely."

All the better to lure a husband.

Cecilia gritted her teeth and followed her mother toward the door.

Her mother paused with her hand on the latch and turned her head to look back at Cecilia. "I forgot to mention there will be a Yule log hunt tomorrow. You will be paired with Cosford."

Cecilia was glad she'd stopped too, or she might have tripped. "Why must I be paired with him? Indeed, why must I be paired with anyone?"

"Because that's what Mrs. Beverley has arranged. And you will not make trouble about it," her mother added sternly. "I don't want Mrs. Beverley to think you rude."

"Of course not." It wasn't possible anyway, not when the Menace was in possession of every bit of rudeness available in the world. "Will we be chaperoned?" Cecilia asked.

"Yes, one of your friends will chaperone since all of them are married." It wasn't a clear jab, but the subtle insinuation was there—that Cecilia ought to be wed too.

"Still, we'll be wandering around in a forest. It seems there would be a potential for compromise." Cecilia frowned. "Are you trying to ensure we are forced to wed?"

The baroness exhaled. "No. I wouldn't ever force you. Now stop trying to find a way out of this. You're pairing with him tomorrow, and that's the end of it."

Fine, then she'd make him miserable.

Cecilia stifled a smile. Causing him distress would be incredibly diverting. It would also ensure there would be no marriage. She'd remind him of how much they loathed one another—as if he'd forget. Chances were, he wouldn't want to be paired with her any more than she wanted to be with him.

Still, she could take the opportunity to needle him, at least a bit.

She trailed her mother down the stairs to the ground floor and into the large gathering hall. Tall windows looked out to the courtyard in the center of the house. Cecilia's bedchamber had a view of the same space.

As soon as she stepped inside, three young ladies came toward her. One was Dinah, and the others were Eleanor Mainwaring and Sophia Priestly. They greeted Cecilia warmly, and she realized she was the only unmarried young lady there. Wait, was that true? She glanced around the room and didn't see any other unmarried women. Mrs. Beverley's widowed mother didn't count.

That meant the only match Cecilia could make at this party was with Cosford. If he didn't already know that was the intent, he would surely puzzle it out. Unless he was as empty-headed as he was malicious.

Cecilia moved with her friends to the side of the room. "I am relying on all of you to protect me from my mother's matchmaking. She wants me to consider the Menace, and I refuse."

"Because of what he did five years ago," Sophia, a young white woman with pale blonde hair and blue eyes, said with a nod. "I don't blame you. He's abhorrent."

"The Menace is a person?" Eleanor asked, her brow puckered in confusion. A Black woman, she was tall, with nearly black hair and expressive, deep brown eyes.

"Oh, yes," Cecilia said. "He's a reprehensible man who ruined two—two!—of my gowns at a house party five years ago."

Eleanor wrinkled her nose. "He *sounds* like a menace."

Sophia tipped her head. "Pity, because he's incredibly handsome. And wealthy."

"Not to mention, you'd be a countess and a *duchess* someday." Dinah scanned the room. "There he is. With Spetch."

Cecilia looked toward Dinah's husband, a white man with light brown hair and a thin face. The white man next to him—the Menace—was taller than she recalled and more...muscular. He wore a stylish green velvet coat. His dark brown hair was pulled back into a queue. He laughed at something Spetch said, his lips spreading to reveal even white teeth and a thoroughly irritating dimple. She didn't remember that detail at all, but perhaps it was because she only recalled him scowling or smirking.

He turned his head so she could see his face full-on. Dammit, he *was* handsome. He had long, dark lashes and cheekbones that looked as if they'd been carved by an expert sculptor.

Turning away from him, she took a deep breath. He could be as attractive as the winter was cold and wealthier than the king. That changed nothing. She also didn't give a fig about his titles. "I've no interest in becoming his countess," she said to her friends. "I'm relying on you to keep me safe from his machinations. Who knows what he has planned?" And they were supposed to go into the forest together tomorrow? Cecilia would be on her guard.

"If he has a scheme, we'll discover it," Dinah vowed. "Spetch will tell me everything."

Cecilia nodded at her. "Good." In the meantime, Cecilia would concoct her own plan—one that would keep him away from her forever.

CHAPTER 2

*J*ohn Rowley, the Earl of Cosford, recognized Miss Cecilia Bromwell the moment she stepped into the hall, despite the fact that five years had changed her considerably. The girl of fifteen had matured into a beautiful woman. Blonde curls fell against the left side of her neck, drawing his attention to the graceful sweep of her collarbone. Delicate brows arched over round eyes that turned up at the corners. She was white, her skin a shade paler than the rich ivory of her gown. Her lush lips pursed ever so slightly just before she walked to the side of the room with her friends. Then she turned her back on him.

Timothy Arbuckle, Baron Spetchley and John's oldest friend, blew a soft whistle through his teeth. "I didn't know Cecilia Bromwell was going to be here. Did you?"

"Yes." John's parents had informed him last night.

"And you still came?" Spetch laughed.

"I didn't have a choice." John kept his voice low. "Apparently my father and her father have been…negotiating."

Spetch's blue eyes widened. "Marriage?"

John responded with a single slow nod.

"You can't want that," Spetch said.

"Not particularly. She's a shrew."

"She came to my wedding when you didn't." Spetch's tone was slightly accusatory.

"I can't help that I was traveling." John had just returned from Italy about six weeks ago. "You could have waited."

"For you?" Spetch shook his head. "Tell that to my darling wife. In any case, Miss Bromwell was quite charming, actually."

John scowled at him. "I'm sure it was an act. She had to be on her best behavior for her friend's wedding."

"Or perhaps she reserves her worst behavior for you."

Grunting, John took a sip of madeira.

"So, you're going to marry her?" Spetch asked.

"Not if I can help it. But my father is adamant this is an excellent match. They want to sign a marriage contract before the party is over, and we'll wed in the new year." John's shoulder twitched. "I'm hopeful there will be other unmarried young ladies here. Any of them will be preferable to the Shrew."

"Well, good luck to you, Cosford. Though, I can't say I've seen any young ladies fitting that description aside from Miss Bromwell."

John tamped down a growl and took another drink.

"Don't fret," Spetch said. "I can't imagine Miss Bromwell wants to wed you any more than you want to marry her. Your parents will have to accept that you do not suit."

"Yes. Exactly that." John breathed a little easier.

Of course she would resist this as much as he would.

He glanced toward her. Her back was to him, but he heard her laugh. One of the other young ladies darted a look at him. Were they discussing him? No, the Shrew wouldn't give him the satisfaction.

Michael Priestly joined them, his gilded hair shining in the candlelight. "I've just learned there will be a Yule log hunt on the morrow. We're to be paired off for a contest to see who can find the largest." He grinned before sipping his wine.

Paired off... John shot another look at the Shrew. Would they be put together? If there were truly no other young unmarried people in attendance, he had to assume that would be the case. Dammit. He looked intently at Priest and Spetch. "Promise me you will not leave me alone with that shrew."

Priest blinked. "What shrew?"

"He doesn't know about her," Spetch said. He turned his head toward Priest. "Miss Cecilia Bromwell—the blonde over there speaking with our wives and Mrs. Mainwaring."

Looking toward the Shrew, Priest blinked. "Why is she a shrew?"

"Because five years ago at this very house, we were all at a house party and she behaved like one," John said tightly. "She ruined my favorite riding boots by filling them with jam. It prevented me from taking a ride I was very much anticipating with Spetch and Main and the other young men who were in attendance."

Spetch smirked at John. "He's leaving out the part where he put a snake in a boat, which caused Miss Bromwell—and my wife—to capsize. We had to jump into the lake and rescue them."

John recalled that horrifying moment. "I didn't realize any of the girls were going to row. I'd intended that snake for you and Main." But his scheme hadn't gone as he'd envisioned, and the Shrew and her friend had climbed into the boat. John hadn't been paying much attention until he heard the young lady who was now Spetch's wife shriek. Then he'd watched in horror as she'd stood in the boat and sent herself and the Shrew tumbling into the lake. Without hesitation, he'd thrown off his boots—the very ones the Shrew ruined the next day—and coat and dove into the water. Spetch had done the same.

While Spetch's quarry had proven difficult to save, due to her splashing about with terror, John had easily caught hold of the Shrew.

"I'm sorry about the snake," he said.

Her eyes, a lovely sherry brown, narrowed on him like a predator sighting its prey. "That was you?"

"Er, yes. It was supposed to be a joke for my chums."

"Oh, that was hilarious for certain." Her sarcasm dripped over him like water from the lake.

"I'm terribly sorry you fell in."

"You ruined my dress. And I can't even swim to the shore in this bloody thing."

"You can swim?" He found that shocking.

"Of course I can." She spoke haughtily, angrily, her eyes ablaze with fury. She was quite pretty in spite of that.

He started towing her toward the shore. "I'd like to see you swim."

"Why, because you don't believe me?" She scoffed. "Should I expect you to put another snake in my boat? I won't fall for that a second time. Or perhaps you'll simply push me into the water next time. If you think I'm coming anywhere near this lake for the rest of this house party, your brains are mush."

"I told you I didn't do it on purpose."

"You did *do it on purpose. I was just the wrong victim. It was a nasty prank, and it failed spectacularly. I should hope you've learned your lesson."*

"What lesson is that?"

Her cold, furious stare settled on him. "That if you wish to target someone, don't miss."

He should have given more credence to her words. She'd targeted him the next day, and her aim had been blisteringly true. In a way, he had to admire her. At least in retrospect. At the time, he'd been irate.

"So, you capsized her boat, and she retaliated with jam in your boots," Priest summarized. "Sounds fair."

"But that wasn't the end of it," Spetch said. "Later, after the boot incident, Cosford confronted her. She told him he got what he deserved. He tried to argue that he hadn't intended to make her fall into the lake. She said it didn't matter, that the damage to her—and to Dinah—was done. She said they were even."

John recalled what happened next. It hadn't been his finest moment.

"Even?" he demanded. "I didn't mean to harm you in any way, but you ruined my boots and made it so I couldn't ride with the others."

She tilted her head and gave him a sickly sweet smile. "Poor you."

"Even would be if I did something specifically to you. Such as this." John grabbed the pitcher of lemonade from the table at which she sat with her friends and dumped it over her head.

That had made her shriek. It had also drawn the attention of the other ladies in the room, including her and John's mothers. John had been made to apologize, but he hadn't meant it.

He glanced in her direction once more. Perhaps he ought to apologize in earnest.

No! She didn't deserve that. She'd gotten what she deserved. Tit for tat.

They need only suffer through the Yule log hunt and inform their parents that they didn't suit. Surely they could both do that, then they could part ways without further injury.

Committing to his plan, he excused himself from his friends and strode toward her. He could see the faces of the other three ladies with whom she stood, and every single one watched his approach with a wide stare. When he arrived behind the Shrew, er, Miss Bromwell, Spetch's wife, Dinah, gently cleared her throat.

It took a moment, but Miss Bromwell gradually turned. She was even lovelier up close. Her eyes were so wonderfully vivid—John could see the derision glimmering in their depths. He found it strangely alluring. Her nose was just slightly upturned, and her lips were full and pink. Very kissable.

Why the hell was he thinking of her like that? He wanted a truce, not an assignation.

"Good evening, Miss Bromwell," he said evenly. "I wonder if I might have a word?"

"I can't imagine we have anything to discuss, Cosford." Her gaze swept over him, glinting with… something, but when she fixed her attention back to his face, her expression clearly found him wanting.

The three other women departed hastily, which Miss Bromwell noticed. "Traitors," she murmured.

Glad to have her alone, if only briefly, he said, "I assume we both know our parents intend to match us, just as I assume you are as averse to the notion as I am."

"I'd sooner join a convent."

He nearly smiled. "Excellent. Then we need only suffer through tomorrow's Yule log hunt and inform them we don't suit. I suggest a truce."

She arched a pale, slender brow at him. "Are we at war?"

"I am not," he said affably. "I just want to make sure you aren't either."

"It's been five years."

He noted she didn't deny being at odds with him. "Yes, what happened here five years ago is the distant past. I'm sure we are different people now. Do you agree to the truce?"

She lifted a shoulder. "I suppose. So long as we are in agreement that we *do not suit*."

"Quite." Pity, because she was really quite beautiful and, of course, clever. Her ivory gown hugged her curves to perfection, and the ruby pendant glittering against her flesh drew his attention to areas he was better off ignoring. He fixed his attention on her inscrutable face. "You look lovely this evening."

She narrowed one eye at him, as if in disbelief. It was then that he noticed a spider descending toward her shoulder. He reached out to knock it away, forgetting he held a glass of madeira in his hand. The wine splashed down the front of her gown.

Gasping, her eyes met his in horror. "You beast!"

How had he managed to do that? "I didn't do that on purpose! Not like with the lemonade."

"You think I'd believe you? Take your truce and stick it...somewhere unpleasant."

"I am truly sorry, Miss Bromwell." He pulled a handkerchief from his pocket and tried to dab at her front.

She smacked his hand away. "What are you *doing?*"

He realized, far too late, that he'd touched her inappropriately. Could this get any worse? He glanced down at her and saw that her bodice was quite wet. As a result, he could make out features he was not able to a moment ago... "Er, your gown is becoming rather provocative," he whispered.

She glared at him, her eyes sparking with outrage. "You're a menace." She spun on her heel and stalked directly to her mother.

Damn, he'd botched that in the worst possible way. Alas, a truce would be impossible. It might also be unnecessary if she were even now convincing her mother that they could not be paired on the hunt tomorrow.

John could only hope.

CHAPTER 3

*C*ecilia was glad to be able to ride to the hunt in a coach that didn't contain Cosford. That she'd even had to come today at all was a travesty. But she was prepared.

After he'd spilled his wine on her last night, ruining yet *another* gown, Cecilia's mother had tried to soothe her. Cecilia had declared the man unfit for feminine company let alone marriage. She'd refused to attend the hunt if they still intended to pair her with the Menace.

Shockingly, her mother had visited Cecilia's chamber later and informed her that she would indeed still be paired with the Menace and that he was very sorry for the wine-spilling incident. Cecilia had known better than to rail against her mother. Instead, she'd plotted her revenge.

Until he'd publicly embarrassed her yet again, she'd been glad to go along with his plan to simply endure their time together and then inform everyone they didn't suit. It would have been easy. But she simply couldn't let him go unpunished.

To that end, she would ensure he lost himself in the forest today. She'd painstakingly removed gold beads from one of her gowns and would drop them to mark their path. When she was sure she and the Menace were sufficiently removed from everyone else—and hopefully lost—she'd steal away from him and retrace their path.

She didn't worry that he'd be stuck outside all day. He would surely find his way back. Eventually.

"You've been awfully quiet," Dinah observed as the coach drew to a halt at the edge of the forest.

"Have I?" Cecilia was eager to depart and execute her scheme.

The door to the coach opened, and a footman helped all four ladies down. The gentlemen stood nearby as did a group of other guests from the party. All told, there were a dozen people, though Cecilia's parents were not among them. Neither were the Duke and Duchess of Ironbridge, the Menace's parents.

Their host, Mr. Beverley, stepped forward and commanded everyone's attention. "As you know, we are on the hunt for Broadheath's Yule log! The bigger the better, so there will be a contest as to who finds the largest tree to fell. Go forth and return within the hour. It may snow later, and we don't want to get caught in a storm."

"What do we win?" Priest called out.

"Bragging rights," Mr. Beverley responded.

"That's hardly a prize," Dinah said.

Cecilia would earn something far better: sweet revenge against the Menace.

"Now, everyone should take one of the baskets," Mr. Beverley said. "There is food and ale in case you become peckish on your quest."

"I wonder if I might have a brief word?" Cecilia asked Dinah. Before they'd left the house, Dinah had informed her that she and her husband would be acting as chaperones to Cecilia and the Menace. They'd both laughed since Cecilia was actually several months older than Dinah. Society's rules were so absurd.

Dinah took several steps away from the group with Cecilia. "Is something wrong?"

"Not at all. I have a plan for the Menace today, and the execution will fail if you and Spetch are with us."

"That's why you were so quiet in the coach. You were plotting!" Dinah's eyes gleamed with anticipation. "I'll ensure we're separated somehow." She blinked in mock innocence.

Cecilia grinned. "Perfect."

Picking up one of the baskets, Dinah peered inside. "There's ale. Just dump it on the Menace before he gets a chance to spill it on you."

After laughing at her friend's jest, Cecilia waited until all the baskets had been taken except the last one. Everyone had paired off, leaving her and the Menace eyeing each other warily. Lifting her chin, she strode to the basket and picked it up.

He met her there. "Do you want me to carry it?"

She supposed she ought to let him have it since he would hopefully be lost by himself for a period of time. "If you like." She set it back down rather than hand it to him.

Sweeping the basket up, he met her gaze with a grimace. "I am sorry for last night."

"So you've said."

"You don't believe me?"

"Does it matter what I believe? The damage was done, regardless of your intent. You are simply bad luck."

He actually laughed, the *menace*. "Is that what I am? What if you are the bad luck?"

"Only in your presence," she murmured. "Which is why I'm not enthusiastic about our pairing today. Let us get through it as quickly as possible."

"We could just stay here," he suggested.

She would absolutely have taken him up on that prior to last night's debacle. "No, we must demonstrate our attempt to get to know one another. How else can we tell our parents with certainty that we do not suit?"

He exhaled. "You make a good point. Come along, then." He started off toward the forest, then stopped abruptly and glanced about. "We're supposed to go with Spetch and his wife. Where did they go?"

Cecilia pointed in a direction no one else had gone. "They started off that way, I believe. We should catch up." She led him along the edge of the forest for several minutes and then ventured into the trees.

"Spetch and I plan to find the largest tree," he said. "I want to win."

She sent him a sidelong glance as he moved to walk beside her. "Even though there is no real prize?"

"The notoriety is enough for me."

Now Cecilia laughed softly. "That doesn't surprise me."

"*That* doesn't surprise me either."

"It seems we may know more about each other than we thought," she said. "That is also surprising, since we didn't get to know each other five years ago."

They walked in silence in the trees for a few minutes. The scent of pine and damp earth filled the air, and a natural wintry quiet settled over them. She slid her hand into her pocket and pulled out a handful of gold beads. Surreptitiously, she dropped them at intervals on the side opposite from where he walked next to her.

"I regret that we didn't meet properly," he said, breaking the peace as they stepped into a wide clearing. "The boat incident happened early enough in the house party that I hadn't yet formed an acquaintance with you."

She didn't believe his remorse for a moment. "We were introduced."

"Yes, but I didn't spend time with you. If I recall, you girls clung together."

"Just as you young men were inseparable. I recall you whinging at length about missing your precious ride with them."

He dipped his head. "I would hardly call it whinging. I was peeved."

"Peeved is far more dignified than you were. *Peeved* people don't toss pitchers of lemonade over others' heads, particularly young ladies who are minding their own business."

"Putting jam in my boots is your business?"

"On that day, it was. You had it coming." She waved her hand. "There's no point revisiting it. Let us just get through this hunt."

"Where the devil did Spetch and Dinah go?" he asked, frowning.

"They have to be nearby." Picking up her speed, she walked ahead of him.

She continued to walk quickly as they reentered the trees on the other side of the clearing, counting on his competitive nature to make him stride past her, which would allow her to get away. But first, she needed to make sure they were far from everyone else. She continued to drop beads to mark their path.

They maintained their brisk pace for some time,

a quarter hour at least, she would guess. She was beginning to feel fatigued, so she decided to slow down. The part of her that liked to win bristled against letting him get ahead of her. However, she reminded herself that she would win in the end.

"Tired?" he asked over his shoulder a few minutes later. "We can stop to rest, if you need to. I think we've completely lost Spetch and Dinah. And everyone else."

She needed to keep him going. "I see larger trees up ahead."

He quickened his pace, and she took the chance to walk even more slowly. She did this for several minutes, continuing to drop beads until he was nearly out of sight amidst the trees. It began to snow lightly. If she was going to execute her plan, she needed to do it now.

Moving quickly, she dashed back the way she'd come, nearly running until a stitch in her side forced her to slow. The snow was coming down more heavily, but the cover of trees was thankfully keeping it from covering her bead path. Finding them was becoming difficult, however, as the day darkened due to the thick cloud cover overhead.

At last, she reached the clearing. But then she stopped cold. Without trees, the ground was completely covered with white. How was she to find her bead path?

Looking across the clearing, she tried to determine from whence they'd emerged. It was impossible to tell. She could pick her way across the snow, which would thoroughly dampen her boots, and try to find the path, or she could go back to find the Menace and hope he recalled the way.

She didn't like either of those choices. Blast!

Setting her anger aside, she counseled herself to do what made the most sense, not what her pride demanded. That meant going to look for the Menace. And what if she couldn't find him? Her bead path would take her only so far. Presumably, he'd kept going. Had he even realized she was gone?

She'd soon find out. Hopefully. Because if she didn't find him and it kept snowing like this, she was going to be in trouble.

CHAPTER 4

The falling snow grew heavier. John tipped his head back and got a snowflake in his eye for his trouble. Wiping at his eyelid, he wondered if they ought to turn back.

"You're awfully quiet." John stopped and turned to look for the Shrew. Was he back to calling her that? Apparently. Why she agitated him was a mystery. He was typically amiable and even charming. But for some reason, she provoked him.

She was no longer behind him. Had she taken a rest? He could see her refusing to tell him that she needed to stop.

Taking a deep breath and shaking his head, he retraced his steps and looked for her red skirts that were visible beneath her dark blue cloak when she walked. The ground was speckled with white as some snow found its way through the trees.

After a while, he stopped and frowned. He set the basket down and looked back from whence he'd come, then turned in a circle. He'd been about to yell, "Shrew." Rolling his eyes at himself he called, "Miss Bromwell? Miss Bromwell?"

Where had she gone? How had she managed to lose herself when she'd been behind him?

Picking up the basket, he continued back the way they'd come. At least he thought it was the way they'd come. He was rather hopeless with direction, not that he would ever admit it.

"Miss Bromwell?" He heard rustling. Then what sounded like muttering. Rather than call her name again, he kept moving—stealthily—in the direction of the noise.

When he caught sight of her, he stopped and listened intently. She was swearing. Rather colorfully. He couldn't stop the grin that rose to his lips.

She turned toward him, but he hadn't made a sound. "What are you smiling at?"

He stepped toward her, swinging the basket. "Are you lost?"

She put a hand on her hip. "Are you?"

"I was looking for you. You were supposed to be right behind me." He paused and tilted his head, contemplating her. "How does one get lost following another person?"

She scowled at him, her brow as dark as the sky was becoming. "I am not lost. I am looking for you. *You* are lost."

She wasn't wrong, but he wasn't going to tell her so. "How is it that you had to look for me when I was right in front of you?"

A low growl rent the air, and for a moment he worried there was a wolf nearby. Then he realized the sound came from her. She put her other hand on her other hip and faced him, her eyes narrowing angrily. "I *tried* to lose you. I had a magnificent plan to abandon you in the forest, but this snow has ruined—"

"*Stop.*" He stared at her. "Explain your *idiotic* plan."

She sniffed. "It was actually quite brilliant. I left a trail of beads that would lead me back to the coaches. After I led you far enough away from them and everyone else, I would make my way back alone."

He continued to glower at her in silence. When she twitched her shoulders and began to look mildly uncomfortable, he relaxed slightly.

"You would have found your way back," she murmured.

He didn't share her confidence since he was generally rubbish with direction. But he wouldn't give her the satisfaction of knowing that. "I'm not sure how, since you thought we'd be deep enough into the forest that you would need beads to find your way." He had to admit it was rather clever of her. "While this scheme is more sophisticated than jam in my boots, I daresay the results are less favorable, since you will suffer the consequences along with me."

She grimaced. "Perhaps the plan wasn't quite as brilliant as I thought. I did not count on it snowing."

He set a hand on his hip and looked around. "So, you've no idea how to find the coaches?" He sure as hell didn't.

"Unfortunately, no."

He noted that parts of her cloak were turning white with snow. She'd soon be quite wet. As would he. "We'd best try to find our way back." Turning, he started to walk.

"Not that way," she said. "You came from that direction."

Dammit, she was right. He gestured with his hand. "Then you lead the way."

"I can take you back to the clearing. Perhaps you can determine where we crossed it."

He wouldn't bet on it. But what choice did they have?

She stalked past him, keeping her gaze trained straight ahead. After several minutes, she stopped short and spun to face him. "This doesn't look familiar. You've made me disoriented."

"This is *my* fault? I'm not the one who planned to abandon the other person in the forest in December."

She stared at him. Coldly. "How did you plan to find your way back once we found the log?"

"Er... I thought we'd be with Spetch. And that the others would be within earshot." That had been John's plan anyway, since he was easily turned around.

"You have no idea where to go?" She crossed her arms over her chest.

He looked around and had no inkling. "No more than you, apparently."

"We are truly lost, then."

"And wet."

She wrapped her arms around herself. "We're going to freeze to death."

For the first time since their acquaintance, she looked vulnerable. He stepped toward her. "Don't be afraid. We'll find our way back. Or we'll find shelter. Perhaps there's a woodcutter's cottage or some other shelter nearby." He would cling to that hope.

He took her hand and started to walk. Only she didn't walk with him. She stared at where he held her. "Why did you do that?"

Letting her go, he shrugged. "I don't know. Come on." He led her up a slope, hoping they'd see the way back. Instead, he saw a roof in the distance. He pointed. "There, do you see it?"

She nodded. "Yes. Let's hurry." She started walking very quickly toward the structure.

John had no notion if she was any good with

direction, but decided she was likely better than him, so he followed her. Ten or so minutes later, they entered a small clearing. The snow came up over his boots and would surely wet the lower parts of her clothing. He considered picking her up, but if taking her hand had caused her alarm, sweeping her into his arms would almost certainly spark distress.

He hurried to the small cottage, praying the door was unlocked and that there was wood for a fire inside. Thankfully, the door pushed open.

"Dare I hope there is furniture?" she asked as he held the door for her.

He'd forgotten to pray for that too. Ah well, he'd settle for a roof over their heads and a fire.

Closing the door firmly, he saw that the cottage was a compact, single room. There was, in fact, furniture—a small table, a single chair, and a narrow bed. He set the basket on the table. "At least we have food."

"There's no wood," she said. "You're going to have to cut down a tree. Is there an axe?"

By the time he could fell a tree and cut it into useable wood, she might very well be freezing. "I'll look outside for wood."

He ducked out and found some stacked against the side of the cottage. There wasn't a great deal, but it would be enough, even if they ended up staying overnight. He tried not to think of that happening.

The snow was falling quite heavily now. He hurried to carry several loads of wood inside. When he came in for the last time, he noticed she had laid the fire and was working to get it started.

He swept off his hat, unintentionally sending droplets flying, and set it on the table. "Do you need help?"

"I don't think so." She stood, and the fire flickered in the hearth. The stone fireplace took up most of one of the shorter walls of the rectangular-shaped cottage.

Now he had to admire her fire-building skills. Miss Bromwell was a surprising woman. She was also shivering.

"Here, you need to get out of your wet clothing. Give me your cloak." John held out his hand.

She pursed her lips. "Are you trying to disrobe me? I knew you were a scoundrel, but I didn't realize you were *that* kind of scoundrel."

John nearly hurt himself to keep from rolling his eyes. "I'm trying to ensure you don't catch cold. You need to take off your cloak at least. But I see your gown is also wet. You should remove that too. You can cover yourself with a blanket." He glanced toward the bed.

"There's just one. Blanket," she clarified. "In case you thought to do the same."

"I'll be fine." His greatcoat seemed a bit thicker than her cloak. Still, he was quite damp, particularly after fetching the wood. Shrugging out of the greatcoat, he hung it on one of the many hooks on the wall near the door. They appeared to be the only way in which whoever used the cottage could organize their clothing, for there was no dresser or armoire or even a trunk.

He turned from hanging his garment to see that she'd removed her cloak. Instead of giving it to him, however, she moved past him and hung it on the farthest hook from his greatcoat. Then she removed her jaunty fur-trimmed hat and set it on another hook.

"You'll need to turn around," she said pertly as she went to the bed.

"Do you mind if I face the fire? I won't stand

directly in front of it." He wouldn't take all the heat.

"Do what you will." Was she going to be disagreeable the entire time they were trapped together?

John decided to remove his coat since its shoulders were also damp. After hanging it next to his greatcoat, he went to the fire, presenting his back to Miss Bromwell.

Several minutes went by. She muttered something, sounding frustrated.

"Do you need help?' John asked. He'd helped a number of ladies disrobe and knew it could be challenging for them without assistance. Miss Bromwell certainly had a maid who helped her dress and undress.

"No," she snapped. "Thank you," she added in a more moderate tone.

A few more minutes elapsed, during which she continued to mutter. They were curses, he realized.

"Oh, fine. I need your help." She sounded most exasperated. "You may turn around."

When he did so, it was to see that she had her back to him. Her dress was partially unlaced, and the laces were knotted. "I see the problem. I'll free you in a trice."

John stepped behind her and began to work at the knot.

"My hands are too cold," she said.

"Here, move closer to the fire." He put a hand on her waist and nearly jumped back at the jolt of awareness that raced up his arm. Ignoring the sensation, he guided her to the hearth. "Warm your hands."

She faced the fire while he went back to work on her gown. "Thank you. This is very awkward."

"Yes." Despite his best efforts, he couldn't stop

thinking of the way his body had reacted to touching her—as if they were magnetized. He hadn't wanted to let her go, and yet it was absolutely necessary he do so.

He was thankfully able to get the laces unknotted. "There. I'll go back to the fire." He turned, stepping around her, and faced the hearth.

She was still there, and her gaze met his—with surprising gratitude. "I appreciate your help."

"I hope you'll let me know if I can provide further assistance."

Giving him a slight nod, she turned and disappeared from sight. He heard her walking across the floorboards, and a moment later, she was next to him once more, the blanket wrapped around her shoulders, covering her undergarments. Mostly. He could see the front of her waist where the blanket didn't meet because she was holding it together higher up over her bosom. He could also glimpse her neck, which had been mostly covered by her gown. The garment had buttoned nearly to her chin.

They stood in silence for several minutes as warmth seeped into them. At length, she said, "I should take off my boots. They are rather wet."

He didn't want her to move away from the fire. Glancing around the cottage, he thought about moving the chair to the hearth, but then only one of them would be able to sit. However, if he moved the bed in front of the fireplace, they could both sit upon it and be close to the heat.

"Just a moment." He went to where the bed stood against the wall and scooted it parallel to the hearth.

"What are you doing?"

"Giving us both a place to sit in front of the fire."

"Well, that's clever."

John froze. "Hold. Is that…approval I hear?"

"It is an observation, nothing more." She sat on the edge of the bed and leaned down to pluck the laces of her boots. When she was finished, she removed them both and set them to the side of the fireplace so they would dry.

Picking up the food basket from the table, John brought it to the bed and set it between them as he sat down. It would provide a nice barrier, which he thought was necessary. Not just because he was feeling a pull toward her, but because he would wager that she wanted something to separate them.

"How long do you think the storm will last?" she asked.

He looked toward the small, single window situated over the table on the same wall as the door. It was snowing so heavily that he couldn't see outside. "There's no telling. It looks quite bad, however. I wonder what happened with everyone else."

She turned her head toward him, her eyes wide. "Do you think they'll find us? If we're found together like this…" She pressed her lips together in a grim line.

He finished her sentence in his mind: *We'll be forced to wed.*

"I have to think we are, unfortunately, rather far removed from everyone else. But then my sense of direction is somewhat worthless."

"I gathered that," she said wryly, seeming to be amused with him rather than at him. Was this progress? Was there a chance they might emerge from this no longer loathing one another?

"I will hope they all made it back to the coaches and are on their way to Broadheath."

"Without us?" she asked, sounding surprised. "I would think they would look for us at least."

"It would be extremely difficult to do so in this storm."

"My mother is going to have a fit," she murmured, letting go of the blanket to hold her hands to the fire.

Without her hands to hold the blanket together, the wool gaped and revealed her corset. The garment was very pretty, with embroidered flowers that seemed pointless on an undergarment. He tried not to look at the swell of her breasts pushing over the top of the corset and failed miserably. He jerked his head toward the fire.

"I hope we aren't here overnight. That really will be a death knell." She added, "As far as compromise, I mean."

If he had to spend the night here with her, they were most definitely doomed. They would have to keep warm, and there was just one bed and one blanket. Even if nothing happened between them—and nothing *would*—the assumption would be that it had.

John fervently hoped the storm would end soon.

CHAPTER 5

*C*ecilia tried not to think of the fact that she was sitting on a bed with a gentleman she was supposed to wed but did not want to.

Alone in a cottage.

In the middle of a snowstorm.

Partially undressed.

This was a disaster. And it was all her fault.

Was it? It seemed they'd always been in danger of getting lost on their hunt since the Menace was apparently terrible at finding his way.

"I'm sorry my beads weren't able to lead us back," she said softly.

"I am too. You were smart to use them, even if it was for nefarious purposes."

Cecilia laughed. "Aren't you angry?"

"My survival instinct outweighs my outrage. Now, as I'm sitting here with you trapped in this tiny cottage, I think it's perhaps best if we try to get along instead of glare at each other in stony silence."

She couldn't find fault with that, as much as she might want to. "I hope you're not asking me to forget the past. I'm willing to set it aside for now, but we aren't ever going to be friends."

"No, I shouldn't think so, especially after last night."

Angling herself toward him, she clutched the blanket in front of her chest once more. "You admit you did that on purpose, then?"

"Absolutely not. I just don't expect you to ever believe me. I truly was trying to knock a spider away." He held up his finger to punctuate his point. "Which I did, I might add."

"I should consider you my gallant rescuer? I am no more afraid of spiders than I am snakes."

"I don't suppose you are," he said sardonically. "Should we eat?"

"We may as well." The contents were wrapped in a cloth, which she opened. Too bad it wasn't larger so it could be used as a second blanket. "There's bread, cheese, ham, and some dried fruit. And ale." Cecilia broke off some cheese and took a slice of bread from the basket. "Help yourself."

He reached in and withdrew some fruit. They ate in silence for a moment. When he'd finished what he'd taken, he looked back into the basket. "No jam?"

Cecilia had just taken a bite of bread and cheese and nearly choked. She didn't want to find him amusing, but he was surprising her.

"What made you decide on jam in my boots?" he asked pleasantly, as if this were an ordinary conversation two people might have at any social gathering.

"I knew it would prevent you from riding. It seemed fitting since you prevented me from engaging in any activities the rest of the day after I fell into the lake. When I returned to the house, my mother made me stay abed to ward off a chill."

He blinked at her. "It was a warm day."

"The lake was not. Warm, that is. Which you should recall since you came to my aid."

"I don't remember the temperature of the water. I do remember being surprised—and impressed—that you could swim."

"Please do not compliment me. It's bad enough I have to accept your help and company." She didn't want to like him. "Anyway, my mother felt it necessary that I rest after my 'ordeal in the lake,' and I missed all the fun that afternoon and evening, including the parlor games."

Grimacing, he pulled the bottle of ale from the basket. "I hadn't thought of that. My apologies. Truly. You were right. It *was* a nasty prank, and I shouldn't have done it."

She stared at him as he opened the ale. "You aren't really taking accountability for that."

"I am. I hadn't intended to cause harm, but I can see now that it was almost guaranteed. I am glad you weren't hurt."

"Beyond my pride," she said with a snort.

"Did you just snort?"

"Bad habit, I'm afraid. My mother detests it." She cast him a sidelong glance before taking another bite of bread and cheese.

"There aren't any cups for the ale, unfortunately. And our lodgings are woefully bereft of comforts such as utensils or drinking vessels."

"I shall complain to the landlord," Cecilia said with a small smile.

"Yes, do that. While you're at it, tell him the furnishings are also lacking. Only *one* blanket?"

"Are you cold?" Perhaps she ought to share the blanket. "You can have a turn." She started to remove the wool from her shoulders, but he held up his hand.

"Probably best if you keep that around you, at

least until your cloak is dry and you can use that instead."

Cecilia glanced toward where their garments hung. "They would be better by the fire, but I don't know where we would place them."

"It's more important we remain warm." He swigged ale from the bottle, then offered it to her.

She stared at the bottle, her pulse moving faster than it had a moment before. Then she lifted her gaze to his. "I'm to put my mouth where yours was?"

Small circles of red bloomed in his cheeks. "I didn't think of that. As I said, there are no cups."

Taking the bottle from him, she willed the tremor racing through her body to still. "We're already sitting here in a state of undress on a bed together. Anyway, it's not as if you're putting your mouth actually *on* mine."

Heavens, now she was thinking of that. She'd kissed precisely one man last Season. They'd been in the shadows in the garden at some ball or other —the event was so unremarkable that she couldn't even recall where it had happened. Everyone, including her now-married friends, always talked about the pleasures of kissing, but Cecilia had yet to experience it. That hadn't stopped her from drawing out the details of kissing as well as other acts. She certainly wasn't going to get that information from her mother, and it was important for a woman to know these things in advance of marriage. Otherwise, she'd have to rely on her husband for tutelage, and that seemed a poor situation indeed.

"Where has your mind gone?" the Menace asked.

"I should really stop thinking of you as the Menace," she said before fastening her mouth precisely where his had been and taking a drink of ale. Her lips and tongue were now where his had been. Another tremor danced through her.

He laughed. "You call me the Menace?"

"It fit you perfectly five years ago, and I find it still resonates."

"Ah, well, I confess I have called you the Shrew since that party."

"You...*menace*!" She set the bottle on the floor and smacked him in the arm. Then she tried very hard not to smile.

He rubbed his biceps. "Ow. You're stronger than you look. I should have made you help me with the wood."

"That would have been more in keeping with your ungentlemanliness."

"I'm not like that," he said quietly, frowning. "Well, I suppose I am with you." He met her gaze. "You provoke me in ways no one else does."

She looked into his hazel eyes—they were really quite captivating—and found she couldn't tear her attention away. "Oh." For some reason, his stare made her even more aware of her lips having been where his were, and they tingled.

Quickly, she shoved the rest of the bread and cheese into her mouth and jerked her gaze to the fire. After swallowing, she asked, "Where did you find that snake?" It was best if they kept talking, especially about things that might prick her ire so she would stop feeling so...drawn to him.

"I went to the lake an hour or so before we were due to meet for the picnic and boating. I found it in the grass and slipped it into one of the boats. I'd planned to direct my friends to that vessel, but you got there first. I didn't for a moment think any of you girls wanted to row."

"Bad assumption."

"So I've now gathered. I shall never underestimate the fairer sex again, especially you."

She flashed him her most provocative smile. "You flatter me, Lord Cosford."

He grinned. "That's Lord *Menace* to you."

All her good humor fled. He was flirting with her. "Please stop."

"What did I do?"

"You're being *nice*."

His dark brows drew together. "I said I preferred that to spending our forced time together at odds."

"Can't you just be...tolerable?" Stifling a moan, she grabbed the ale and took a long drink, then set it back on the floor. "The jam was excessive," she said, keeping her attention on the fire. "Even if you'd meant for *me* to fall into the lake, I should not have retaliated. I have two older brothers, and I'm rather conditioned to give as good as I get."

"Thank you." The words were soft and warm. "*Two* older brothers? That can't have been easy."

"It could be quite challenging, though I will say neither of them put a snake in my boat, bed, or any other place I would happen upon it." Cecilia turned her head toward him and saw he was watching her intently. As if he were intrigued. As if he couldn't look away.

"I can be impulsive," he admitted softly. "Sometimes, I come up with an idea without thinking it through or I react without consideration. That was especially true when I was younger. Hopefully, I've matured. That is why my father sent me to the continent for six months. To, as he said, 'calm my behavior.'"

"And did it work?"

"I'd thought so, but you seem to think I'm every bit as awful as five years ago." He gave her a faint smile, then dug into the basket. Withdrawing a slice of bread with ham, he added, "I wish there was butter."

"Mmm, yes," she murmured, feeling terribly awkward. And perhaps a bit remorseful. "You aren't really as terrible as five years ago. I believe you that there was a spider last night. It seems you're clumsy as well as bad at finding your way."

He let out a loud, sharp laugh that made her smile. "You've puzzled me out completely."

She was suddenly feeling a trifle warm, but she didn't dare put the blanket down. She'd expose far too much of herself.

They were quiet while he finished his ham and bread. He took another drink of ale, and she tried very hard not to think about his mouth now going where hers had been.

He set the bottle back on the floor. "If the jam was excessive, the lemonade was positively beastly. I blame my passionate nature. It was a regrettable moment."

Passionate nature? She reminded herself he was referring to a moment of anger and nothing else.

"You looked furious." She glanced toward him. "In truth, I found you a bit frightening."

"Damn." The word was a bare whisper, but the depth of his remorse was palpable. "Now I am doubly sorry. Triply. *Ugh.* There is no excuse for it. I *was* angry, but that doesn't excuse my behavior."

There was a small crumb on his chin. Without thinking, Cecilia leaned toward him and brushed it away, her fingertips caressing his flesh. His intake of breath sounded like a rifle shot in the small space.

"There was a crumb." She kept her fingers near his mouth, barely touching him, while her mind swirled with uncertainty. What was happening?

Cecilia pulled her hand away and snapped her head toward the fire. "Would you mind checking on the storm?"

"Not at all." He jumped up as if he were aflame.

She crossed her fingers in the hope that the snow had stopped. If it didn't, she began to fear for the worst: that she would indeed *like* him.

CHAPTER 6

*J*ohn couldn't get off the bed fast enough. He'd nearly drawn her fingertip into his mouth, for God's sake. Then he would have sucked and licked her, and his cock would have gone completely hard instead of the half erection he was currently sporting.

He closed his eyes briefly on the way to the window and sent up a silent prayer that it had stopped snowing.

It was snowing harder than ever.

At least it was cooler on this side of the room. He'd just stand there a minute—or ten—until his body came back under control.

This was fast becoming a disaster. Nothing untoward had happened, and it wouldn't. With luck, they'd be able to convince everyone they'd been trapped by the storm and that unfortunate circumstance shouldn't necessitate their marriage. Except, couples had been forced to wed for far less.

And he *was* lusting after her. Shockingly. Impossibly.

Desperately.

She was clever and witty, and she'd owned up

to her mistakes. Was there any reason he should continue to oppose marriage to her?

Wait, was he considering wedding her?

No. No, no, no. He could never wed the Shrew.

But what if she isn't really a shrew?

Of course she wasn't, as he'd just deduced. He massaged his head in the hope that he'd start to think more clearly.

"How's the storm?" she called, interrupting his thoughts and reminding his body that she was still there.

"Would you believe it's worse?" He turned from the window to see that she'd dropped the blanket to her waist.

Looking over her shoulder at him, she scrambled to pull the blanket back up. But not before he saw the pale flesh of her upper back and the plane of her shoulder. He could imagine kissing her there, dragging his tongue along her silken flesh until she quivered in his arms.

This was not helping his cock problem.

John ought to remain by the window, but he was getting cold again. He moved back to the bed, this time situating himself slightly farther away than he had been.

She'd tucked up the food once more, covering it with the cloth in the basket. He reached for the ale and took a swig. He considered offering it to her again, but didn't want another awkward moment of them thinking how they were both drinking from the same place.

"I've been thinking there is probably no way we are going to avoid the parson's trap," she said, her features set into abject disappointment.

He set the bottle back on the floor. "It's likely. I'm sorry."

"I'll fight it." She darted a glance in his direction, her gaze fierce. "Neither of us wants that."

He would have agreed with her at the start of the day, but now? Had his opinion really changed, or was he just thinking with his cock? And if it were, would that be so bad? There were worse reasons to wed.

"Is there no way you could ever be attracted to me?" he asked, trying to inject some levity while also realizing he genuinely wanted to know, since he had apparently done a complete reversal with her.

She whipped her head toward him, her nostrils flaring. "Absolutely not!"

At this point, he saw no reason to prevaricate. They were trapped together, and she *was* compromised. Marriage was probably imminent. "Would it be shocking for you to hear that I find myself attracted to you—both physically and mentally?"

She gaped at him. "Yes. Why?" Waving her hands, she sputtered. "Never mind, I don't wish to know. I realize this situation arouses…temptation. But you must ignore it. If this hadn't happened, if I hadn't been so stupid as to try to make you lost, you would continue to loathe me. Indeed, I don't understand why you don't still. I tried to abandon you in the forest. In December."

She actually managed to provoke his ire a bit. And that made him surprisingly aroused. Sexually. He found he wanted to punish her by showing her how she *could* be attracted to him. He didn't believe her when she said she wasn't. He could see the tic in her throat, the slight tremor in her hands. He supposed she could just be angry, but she'd also revealed that she was very aware of…what had she said?

Temptation.

He blew out a breath. "If you're trying to make me angry, it won't work. It seems I *have* matured. I've already decided I like you. You've a malicious bent, but I think we've established that's only where I'm concerned. Just as my bad behavior has been solely for you. I think that makes our connection rather special, don't you?"

She continued to stare at him, her delectable lips parted. "No, I do not think that. I think you must be wholly unused to unrequited attraction, which I find surprising given how odious you are."

John laughed. She was trying awfully hard to cling to her outrage and her dislike. All it did was support his theory that she was attracted to him in return. "I'm actually quite popular with ladies. You could ask my Italian mistress if she weren't so far—"

"No, thank you. As repellent as I find you, I can believe you are a consummate rake." She narrowed her eyes at him. "That does not recommend you."

He exhaled. "We were getting along so well."

She sniffed. "Until you brought up attraction. It wasn't well done of you."

"You can't say I haven't been a gentleman. I haven't dumped the ale over your head."

"No, you have not."

He caught her smiling—or trying not to smile—and relaxed slightly. "I'll have you know that I am not a rake. I comport myself with adequate propriety and, hopefully, charm. My father demands nothing less."

She gave him an arch look. "Did he really send you to the continent to mature, or perchance to sow your wild oats?"

John laughed. "Probably both. My father did say he preferred I conduct all my misbehavior far away from London. He expects me to participate in government and stand for a seat in the Commons as soon as I'm able."

"Is that what you want?"

"Since I am to be the duke someday and will sit in the Lords, I understand and accept my duty."

She pursed her lips at him. "That's not an answer. Let me ask another way. Are you driven only by duty?"

He thought about that a moment. "Yes. And no. I mean, it's a part of who I am, so I can't ignore it."

"But you draw the line at marrying the woman your parents selected?"

"I suppose I do," he said slowly. "I'd hoped to choose her myself."

"Now, that is something on which we can agree."

"Oh dear, are we friends now?" he asked, smiling.

"Not yet."

Yet. Well, that was promising. "We've put the past to rest, though, haven't we? We've taken responsibility for our actions, apologized, accepted each other's apologies."

She hesitated. "I suppose. That doesn't mean I am ready to accept being forced into marriage with you."

"Nor am I." Although, he was beginning to think it wouldn't be a hardship at all.

"How old are you?" she asked, turning slightly toward him, her hands still clutching the blanket over her bosom.

"Twenty-three." He knew she was twenty. "Why?"

"Seems young for a man to be pushed into marriage."

"My father wants to ensure the male line."

"So, I'll be expected to breed immediately." She

rolled her eyes, and her grip on the blanket loosened. "Wonderful."

John could now see the flesh above her corset. Again, he imagined putting his mouth on her, coaxing moans of delight from her throat as her body strained against his.

He bolted from the bed. "We need more wood."

Practically running from the cottage, he didn't look back.

≈

Cecilia stared at the closed door. What had happened?

"There's plenty of wood," she muttered to herself as she glanced toward the neat stack that he'd placed in the corner earlier.

Furthermore, he'd gone outside without so much as his coat, let alone hat. He would be wet in a trice if the storm was as bad as he said. Then he'd come back in and have to remove even more clothing, and she'd likely have to give him her blanket. So, he'd be wearing less, and she'd be more exposed.

Heat flushed her body, and she was shocked to feel her breasts tingle. She *was* attracted to him, dammit.

He was quite handsome with those alluring hazel eyes and sculpted features. More than that, he looked at her as if she were wine and he was parched with thirst. Or as if she were extraordinary.

He also smelled divine—of sandalwood and spice. She wanted to lean close to him, to invite his embrace and scent to envelop her.

No, she could not want that!

Standing, she went to the window to verify the

continuance of the storm. What if he'd lied to her to keep them together?

Of course he hadn't. The snow was quite thick and falling in earnest. He might be attracted to her, but she would wager it went against his desires. It certainly went against hers.

But why? He wasn't awful. At least, he wasn't awful *today*. They had been having a nice time until he'd identified the growing connection between them. Couldn't they just ignore that?

You're alone with him in a small cottage with half your clothes off.

Perhaps she ought to embrace it, then. He was right—they were as good as betrothed. Her parents would never allow her to talk her way out of marrying him. It seemed she ought to make the best of it. Or try to anyway.

He was certainly taking his time fetching wood.

Cecilia turned from the window as the door opened. Cosford came inside carrying an armful of fuel. She watched as he took it to the existing stack.

"Why did you need to fetch wood?" she asked, unable to help herself.

After setting his burden down, he straightened, running his hand through his damp hair and sending water droplets into the air. "I'd rather go out now than later."

Later. He thought they would be there awhile. Perhaps even overnight. "You should have worn a hat at least." She moved toward him, noting that his waistcoat was wet, as were his shirtsleeves.

"Probably," he muttered.

"Take your waistcoat off and hang it up to dry."

He swung his head to look at her, his eyes glinting and his mouth turned in a slight frown. "I'm not sure that's wise."

"Wise or not, you will catch cold. You should

probably remove your shirt too, but what would we put over you to keep you from getting chilled? I suppose I can give you the blanket while your garments dry. I confess I was quite warm in front of the fire."

Cecilia stepped toward him and let go of one side of the blanket so it slid down her arm and fell behind her back. The cool air surprised her—she wasn't as warm since she'd been standing at the window for a few minutes.

His nostrils flared, and he jerked his attention to her face. "No, don't do that." He exhaled sharply and again swept his hand through his hair, tousling the dark strands in an irritatingly attractive manner. Why couldn't he be revolting? "I went outside because I was overly aroused, and I thought it best if I compose myself."

Desire streaked through Cecilia, making her shiver in a way that had nothing to do with the cold. "You should probably still take off your waistcoat," she murmured. She reached for the blanket behind her to pull the one side back up over her shoulder, but couldn't quite reach it. She was suddenly feeling rather clumsy.

He reached behind her and pulled the blanket up, his thumb brushing the bare flesh of her collarbone. "I'm sorry to make you uncomfortable. This is so damned awkward."

She clutched the blanket around herself and looked up into his eyes. "Don't apologize. This is all my fault."

"In all honesty, we may have gotten lost anyway, especially if you hadn't spread your beads. We should have stayed near the coaches." His expression turned sheepish. "I wanted to find the largest tree."

"Because you're competitive." At his nod, she

nodded too. "Like me."

"Perhaps we have more in common than we realize." He shivered, then made a face. "All right, I'll take off my waistcoat." Unbuttoning the garment, he removed it and went to hang it on one of the hooks.

Cecilia tried not to stare at the way his body moved beneath the linen of his shirt. She could see his muscles and the play of his shoulders as he hung the waistcoat. Before he could turn, she hastened to sit on the bed once more, lest he catch her watching him.

She began to understand why a dash outside into the cold might alleviate the disturbing attraction she felt toward him. "Did it help?" she asked.

He came to sit on the bed—on the other side of the basket dividing them of course. "Did what help?"

"Going outside."

He rubbed his hand along his thigh. Now she was staring at his muscular thigh. "Ah, yes. But I'm afraid the effect was temporary."

Another pulse of heat spread through her, and she turned her attention to the fire. "Oh." She tried not to think of how just the basket separated them or how only a shirt covered his torso. Somehow, she managed the courage to ask the question she didn't really want the answer to: "Do you think we'll be here overnight?"

"I think it's possible." He spoke slowly, almost haltingly, then glanced at her. "Sorry."

She'd expected that answer even as she still hoped they might escape. To what end? They'd already been alone together for a long time. There could be only one conclusion, much to her despair. "So, we're definitely getting married, then."

He turned toward her, his features creasing

with concern. "You sound despondent. I promise I'm not that bad. I won't ever capsize your boat or dump a beverage over your head. I cannot, however, swear that I won't do something clumsy as I did last night with the wine. And we've established that I'm utter rubbish with finding my way. That will have to be your job, I'm afraid."

"You make it sound as if we might be partners, with each of us having responsibilities."

"And why not? I will readily admit there are likely a great many things you can do better than I can."

She angled herself toward him. "Such as?"

"Sew?"

"I can sew passably well. I will concede you probably shoot better than me. What about dancing?"

"I like to dance, but I can be a trifle clumsy." He pursed his lips as she darted a look at the fire. "I hadn't given much thought to my physical ineptitude until now. I'm afraid you're going to have to tell me something you aren't good at so I'll feel better about myself." He grinned at her, and her heart did a little flip.

"Kissing." Good heavens, why had she said that? She certainly hadn't intended to.

His eyes widened. "Have you extensive experience?"

"No. I've only kissed one gentleman, but it wasn't very enjoyable. I must deduce I'm bad at it."

"Or you simply haven't learned how." His gaze fixed on her mouth.

Her lips tingled. She licked the lower one, her tongue resting against it for a slight moment.

Cosford groaned. "You certainly know how to tease."

She sucked in a breath. "I didn't mean to."

"No, I can't imagine you did. You're an inno-cent?" he asked.

She nodded. "I do know what…happens. I made Dinah tell me after she wed Spetch."

His eyes widened in alarm. "Good God, I do not want to hear what my best friend's wife has to say about sexual intercourse. Pardon my language."

Giggling, Cecilia pressed her hand to her mouth. After a moment, she sobered and lowered it to her lap. "No, I don't imagine you do."

He looked at her, his eyes smoldering with a heat that only stoked Cecilia's ever-present arousal. "Would you like me to teach you how to kiss?"

"That presumes you are worthy of teaching me." She gave him a half smile to show that she was joking.

"You *are* a tease," he murmured, his gaze contin-uing to caress her. "How about if I kiss you and if you find the act satisfactory, I can teach you how? Since you judged your prior kiss to be lacking, I believe you'll be able to discern if mine is more to your liking."

Every word he uttered tripped along her flesh, coaxing her desire. She would wager his kiss would be thrilling. She ought to say no, but why, when they would likely be wed? Better to take con-trol of this situation and manage it the best she could.

"All right." Cecilia picked up the basket and set it behind the bed, away from the fire.

"May I kiss you?" He scooted toward her slightly, and she did the same toward him.

"Yes." She closed her eyes and waited.

The bed creaked as he moved closer. His hand gently cupped her face. "Open your eyes, Cecilia."

She did and saw that he was so close. The innermost part of his irises were quite green. "Why? I thought people kissed with their eyes closed."

"Typically, but I don't want you to think of this as something that happens to you. A kiss is something we do together, a shared experience." He caressed her cheek with his thumb. "When this rogue kissed you, did he use his tongue?"

"Yes. It was slimy."

He smiled, and again, her body reacted with a tremor of excitement. "That is unfortunate." His thumb moved down and slid across her lips.

Her breath was coming faster as her heart picked up speed. "What are you doing?"

"Your lips fascinate me. They're so plump and pink. I want to lick and bite them."

She moved her head back slightly. "Bite?"

"Not painfully. I'll show you at the end of the kiss. Ready?"

Unable to speak, she nodded. He lowered his head and brushed his lips across hers. She didn't close her eyes. The feel of him, fleeting though the touch was, careened through her like a runaway horse. Wild. Dangerous. Freeing.

Cecilia realized she was clutching the mattress as if she were trying to keep from falling off a cliff. She released it and flattened her hands. "May I touch you?"

"Please. Do whatever you like." His voice had deepened.

She had no idea what that might be. "I don't want to do the wrong thing."

Another smile flitted across his lips. "You won't. You couldn't, I assure you."

He slid his hand to the back of her head and kissed her again. But this wasn't fast or light. His lips pressed against hers as he cradled her in his palm. She lifted her hands to his shoulders, which were still damp. So she moved them up to his neck and let her fingertips rest against his flesh above his collar.

Her eyes closed as his mouth moved over hers. His other hand slipped under the blanket and clasped her waist.

He lifted his lips from hers and pressed in again from a new angle. This was already infinitely better than that other kiss.

Then his tongue swept into her mouth, and she tensed, expecting not to like it. But she did. The moment his tongue touched hers, a delicious ripple of pleasure streaked through her. There was simply no comparison to her prior experience.

And this was the *Menace*.

He coaxed her to kiss him back, his hand massaging her waist as he licked and thrust into her mouth. She copied his actions with her tongue and grasped the edge of his collar, holding him tightly as she began to lose herself in his wicked embrace.

Wicked?

Oh, yes. This was terribly bad of them. But what else were they to do with their time together? Particularly when they were going to be forced together in the end. Cecilia began to think she wouldn't mind.

His hand moved down to her nape, sending frissons of delight down her spine as his other hand glided to her back, his fingertips pressing into her undergarments. Then his teeth gently closed over her lower lip, pulling on it as he withdrew his mouth from hers.

She opened her eyes slowly, drowsy with desire, to see him watching her, his gaze slitted. "That was a bite?" she asked softly, her voice sounding hoarse as if she hadn't spoken in days instead of several long, spectacular minutes.

"Of a sort." His eyes opened a bit more. "Was that a better kiss, I hope?"

Reluctantly, she released him, letting her hands fall to her lap. "I have to deduce that what I experienced before wasn't even a kiss. What you just did was…sublime. I'm shocked it was you."

He grinned, his hand leaving her head while the other hand rested atop her thigh. "Because I'm a menace?"

"Precisely." Her body thrummed with need. She didn't want to stop. She wanted the hand that he held on her thigh to move. Preferably between her legs. "What do you do after kissing like that?"

He looked down at the bed, chuckling, then pinned her with a dark, sensual stare. "Are you trying to torture me?"

"No. Forgive me, I'm curious. I could tell you what Dinah told me, but you already said—"

He kissed her again, hard and fast, then pulled back laughing. "No, don't do that. I'll tell you. Or I'll show you. Which would you prefer?"

Excitement pulsed through her, making her breasts feel heavy and her sex…throb. It was wholly unsettling while also thrilling. "Since we seem to have nowhere else to go and nothing else with which to occupy ourselves, I would say show me."

He made a guttural sound deep in his throat. "Do you know what you're asking?"

She nodded. Then she reached behind her back and began to loosen the laces of her corset.

His eyes glittered. "What are you doing?"

"Shouldn't I remove my corset at least?"

"You should *not*, but yes."

A laugh leapt from her as she tilted her head. "You contradicted yourself there."

"I am incredibly conflicted. I want nothing

more than for you to take off your corset along with every other garment you are wearing. But I should not want that."

"Wanting is one thing. Doing is another. I think it's fine for you to want that. I suppose I shouldn't *do* it." She hadn't stopped pulling at her stays and now felt the garment loosen. She pulled the sides, widening the gap. Then she wriggled her torso and pulled it off over her head. Setting it on the edge of the bed, she looked back to Cosford. "It seems I did it anyway. I was nearly do—"

He kissed her once more, his hands cupping her face as his mouth moved over hers with a passionate intensity. His palms slid down her neck to caress her collarbones. They continued their downward path until he glided over her breasts. It was the barest touch—his hands skimming over her nipples. They stiffened against her chemise, aching for more of his attention.

She returned his kiss with fervor and put her hands on his shoulders, again forgetting they were damp. She clutched at his neck again and decided his stock was unnecessary. Unfastening it at the back of his neck, she slipped it from him and tossed it behind him. This allowed her to tuck her hands into his shirt, to feel his warm flesh beneath her fingers.

But then his hands were cupping her breasts, and her exploration halted. His thumbs grazed her nipples through her chemise. She gasped into his mouth as sensation overwhelmed her.

He pulled back. "Too much?"

"No." She clutched at his shoulders. "Not enough. I want…more." She looked into his eyes with a certainty that shocked her. "I want everything."

CHAPTER 7

*S*tark lust thrummed through his body. John's heartbeat pounded so loudly in his ears that he couldn't think. Or perhaps that was due to the incredibly provocative way she was looking at him, as if she were desperate for his touch. At least as desperate as he was for hers.

With a will that surprised him, he took his hands from her and made himself scoot back on the bed. This was wrong. He couldn't take advantage of her like this.

She frowned. "What's the matter?"

"We are venturing into territory from which we can't return." He swallowed, his throat dry. Then he recalled the ale next to the bed and plucked it up. He took a long drink before replacing it on the floor.

"Haven't we already done that?" she asked wryly. "Just by being here together, I mean."

Yes, they'd already established that. "There is a very small chance we could convince our parents not to force a marriage. That would also require everyone in attendance at the party vowing they wouldn't tell anyone about us being alone overnight."

"So, we're assuming we'll be here overnight?"

"I think we must." John couldn't see anyone coming out to look for them in this storm. Hopefully, they weren't too worried. His mother was probably frantic, and he could only imagine what Cecilia's parents were feeling. If John were her father, he'd hope she was safe and warm, even if it meant she was compromised. Except did that even matter if the man compromising her was the one you wanted her to wed in the first place?

John shook his head before he went farther down the rabbit hole of his thoughts. "I need to ask, are you ready to commit to marriage? Because if you aren't, I'm moving to the other side of the bed."

He'd also be sleeping on the floor. If he slept. Between the discomfort of not having a bed or bedclothes and his unsatisfied desire, he doubted he would find rest.

A slight frown marred her features, and she looked down at her lap. "I confess that I was hoping to fall in love."

She was a romantic. And she seemed embarrassed by it. "There's nothing wrong with that."

Her head shot back up. "Isn't there? My father certainly finds it annoying."

"He is not a romantic, then," John said.

"Are you?"

John wouldn't have described himself that way. He hadn't thought too much about love. "Probably not. However, I haven't ever met a woman who made me think about such things or who provoked my keen admiration. Until now."

Her eyes widened. "You admire me?"

"For five years now."

She held up her hand with a slight laugh. "Wait.

You admired me when we met before? How is that possible?"

"You said something that stuck with me, that if you're targeting someone, don't miss.'"

"*That* stuck with you?" She laughed again. "I was stating my intent to target you and not miss."

"Which you did with great success. My arrogance prevented me from seeing that." He held his hands out to the fire. The damp shoulders of his shirt gave him an occasional chill. He wondered if he would have been better off removing it. But then he'd be sitting here shirtless. Except, she'd stated her desire to continue their explorations. Did it matter what he was wearing? Or not wearing?

Why was he hesitating? Their fate was all but sealed. That meant they could do whatever they liked. Still, he was reluctant.

Because he'd already begun to care for her. Now that he knew she'd hoped to marry for love, he worried he was consigning her to something she didn't want. He suspected she would likely argue that it was her fault anyway.

Straightening, he addressed her as if they were fully clothed in a drawing room and he was paying a call. "I wonder how things might be if we'd met under different circumstances. Rather, if I had never put that snake in the boat. I remember thinking you were the prettiest girl at the house party five years ago."

"Did you?" She gave him a sly look. "I recall you being the handsomest of the young men. I believe I told my friends that it likely contributed to your arrogance—that you were attractive, and you knew it. And that you probably used it to your advantage."

"To get away with things like capsizing boats?"

"Precisely. I wasn't going to succumb to that, not that looks alone would ever charm me. You certainly didn't exude *actual* charm."

"We weren't there to pair off with any of you. We were all around eighteen, and you were what, fifteen? That's an awkward gap at those ages."

"You were men, and we were girls." She pursed her lips. "However, I'd argue that a fifteen-year-old 'girl' is more mature than an eighteen-year-old 'man.'"

He laughed. "You may be right. I suppose we must accept that our meeting five years ago was likely never going to lead to anything beyond finding each other nice to look at. But if I hadn't put the snake in the boat, you hadn't poured jam in my boots, and I hadn't dumped lemonade over your head, our meeting at this party might have been quite different."

"That is certain. We must presume that our parents would still have tried to match us. Perhaps we would have come to this party interested in getting to know one another."

"Would you have been?" He was surprised to find that he desperately wanted to know—and hoped she would answer in the affirmative.

"It's hard to say. My mother has been trying to match me with one gentleman or another for nearly a year now." She gave him a weak smile. "I admit I was growing weary of her attempts."

"You didn't like any of them?"

"Not enough to wed. I knew I wasn't going to love them. My mother doesn't seem to understand what sort of gentleman I might like."

"Might fall in love with, you mean." He cocked his head. "What sort is that?"

She blew out a breath and looked toward the fire. "I'm not sure I can say explicitly. I suppose I was looking for a...feeling. Some of the gentlemen were nice enough." She looked back at him. "They didn't toss beverages on me."

John winced. "I got off on the wrongest foot. I promise I'm nice and usually a gentleman." He abruptly stood. "Let us pretend we are just meeting for the first time."

Her brows drew together. "Dressed like this?"

"Undressed like this." He grinned. "Imagine we are fully and appropriate garbed." He was having great difficulty with that. Her nipples were quite visible beneath the linen of her chemise, and he was having a devil of a time not fixating on them.

What she said echoed in his mind—that she was looking for a feeling. He suspected he knew what she meant. He felt something quite different after spending this time with her today. Something he'd never felt before.

It was more than desire. It was anticipation. He couldn't wait to discover what happened next between them, whatever that might be.

John executed his courtliest bow. "I am pleased to make your acquaintance, Miss Bromwell."

She inclined her head. "As am I, Lord Cosford."

"Normally, I would ask you to dance or to promenade."

"We'd have to move the bed to dance near the fire. While the cottage has warmed considerably since we've been here, I still prefer to remain close to the heat."

"This is not what people who just met should be talking about." He threw up his hands with a laugh. "I give up. There is no going back. We started terribly, and now we are saddled with one another."

"Is that how you see me? As a burden?" Her voice was small, her features uncertain as she plucked at a thread on the edge of the mattress.

John sat back down, positioning himself right next to her. Then he brought his leg up, bending it at the knee between them so he could face her. "Not at all." He gently caressed her chin. "I see you as someone exciting, an unexpected thrill. Indeed, I think if I'd come to this party without our history, I would have been captivated upon meeting you."

She blinked at him. "Truly?"

"I haven't spent much time contemplating love or any emotion as it pertains to a lady, but with you, I wonder if I've fallen under a spell. Not that love is magic, but—"

"But perhaps it is," she broke in, saying what he was thinking. "Perhaps love is a magic that happens between two very specific people at a specific time. It wasn't there when we met five years ago, but it's here now." She sounded a bit breathless, and it was making him feel the same.

"Yes, I think that's it exactly." He slid his hand along her jaw and cupped her neck below her ear. "I don't know what falling in love feels like, but being with you right now is like nothing I've ever known. You've turned me from utter loathing to abject longing. If I were never to see you again after this, I think I might fall apart."

She sucked in a breath. "What would you do?"

"Pursue you. Relentlessly."

Her eyes glittered with heat. "Then why aren't you now? I told you I wanted everything."

It took everything in him not to clasp her to him and push her back against the mattress. "You're certain you aren't just speaking from arousal? We shouldn't let our bodies command our brains."

"My brain is a part of my body. Does it get to make the final decision?" She leaned toward him and placed her hand on his chest. "My brain is telling me to touch you, to invite you to touch me, to pursue what I think we both want."

"Then you're agreeing to marriage." He had to be sure before they progressed. "Without love. Yet." It was important he add the last part. Because he absolutely thought it was possible.

"Yet." She repeated, flicking the uppermost button on his shirt open. "I am encouraged about our future together."

John's breath caught. His cock, which had been in at least a partial state of arousal for some time now, hardened completely.

He moved toward her, cradling her head and grasping her waist with his other hand. "So we're agreed. We have a future together."

"I think we must. However, I am most concerned with our *immediate* future." She unfastened the other button holding his shirt closed and slid her hand beneath the linen. Her palm flattened against him, and he knew in that moment that she would entice him in ways he hadn't yet imagined.

John stared into her eyes. "Then let us seize it."

CHAPTER 8

*C*osford captured her mouth with his and pushed her back on the bed. Cecilia straightened her legs, and he immediately settled between them. He fitted his hips to hers, and she felt his sex pressing against hers. It was shocking. Sensual. Wonderful.

This was the man she would marry. A man she'd loathed just a few hours earlier. Perhaps that passionate hate wasn't all that distant from a passionate desire, for that was most certainly driving her now. If he'd refused her, she wondered if she might have begged him to reconsider.

Fortunately, he had not. Everything he'd said to her had been surprisingly thrilling. That they agreed this was magical made her heart soar. She might not love him now, but she thought she could. And since she'd never felt that way before, she had to think it was more than possible.

His mouth left hers to kiss a path along her jaw and neck, his lips and tongue igniting sensations that carried through her entire body. She clutched at his head, holding him to her, lest he decide to leave.

He wouldn't do that. For whatever reason, she

trusted that this was indeed what they both wanted. She trusted *him*.

The man who'd done horrible things to her. A giggle burst from her lips.

Cosford lifted his head, one dark brow arching. "This shouldn't be amusing."

"It's not." She caressed his head, loosening the queue at the back. "It's delightful. I just couldn't help thinking that you are the last man I expected to be doing this with."

He smirked. "That part is amusing—and true. Won't we cause a stir with our friends when we inform them that we've changed our minds about each other?"

She laughed again. "Yes."

Lifting her chemise, he skimmed his hand up her rib cage and closed it over her breast. "Now, if you continue to laugh, you will damage my ego. And that may require punishment."

She gasped as he pinched her nipple. "Like that?"

"Perhaps."

"But I liked that. Do it again."

He did as she asked, squeezing and then pulling it so there was just the slightest discomfort.

Sucking in a breath, she dug her fingers into his scalp. "*Again.*"

He pushed the chemise up almost savagely so that the garment covered her face. Then he tugged her nipple again, pressing it between his thumb and forefinger until she moaned. His hand cradled her breast, squeezing it just before his lips closed around her tingling flesh. Lust sparked and raged in her core, making her legs quiver.

Desperate, she worked the chemise over her head and thrust it aside, leaving her clad in only her woolen stockings and garters. She wanted his shirt off too, so she could feel his bare flesh. Sliding her hands down his neck, she tugged at the collar.

He lifted his head, straightening as he whisked the shirt off and cast it away. Cecilia surveyed his chest, from the dark hair in the center to his small, button-like nipples. She flicked her finger over one of them, drawing a gasp from him. "Does that feel as good as what you do to me?"

"I don't know that I can say. Any way you touch me feels spectacular." He held his arms out. "Do what you will."

She tweaked both nipples this time, enjoying the groans he made. Then she brought her hands down over his muscular abdomen where a trail of dark hair disappeared into his waistband. "Where does this go, I wonder?"

"Straight to my cock," he said bluntly, taking her hand and pressing it against his hard shaft through his breeches. "Feel how badly I want you."

"And what will you do with it?" She looked up at him, her sex aching with want.

He leaned down so his mouth was just above hers. "I will slide it into your sex and thrust very deep. Until you cry out my name—John, if you please. Then I'll wrap your legs around me, and I'll drive into you relentlessly until you come. Do you know what that means?"

She nearly whimpered with desire. "I think so. I know there is a…completion. And pleasure. I've… touched myself before. It's never been completely satisfying, though."

"Then let me satisfy you. *Completely*."

He kissed her, his tongue spearing deep into her mouth, making her think that was what he meant to do with his cock. She held him to her, digging her hands into his back as she lifted her hips from the bed to grind herself against him.

Again, he used his teeth on her lower lip, a bit harder this time as he withdrew. He kissed the hollow at the base of her throat as he cupped one breast. She anticipated what came next—his mouth closed over her nipple. But he spent far more time suckling her than before, his lips and tongue drawing on her flesh until she indeed cried out his name.

"You can't be satisfied yet," he murmured as he moved to her other breast and gave it equal attention. With each kiss and lick, she arched higher and trembled harder.

"Take me there, John," she begged.

He licked down her abdomen, his mouth edging closer to her sex. She froze. He couldn't mean to kiss her...there? Dinah hadn't mentioned *that*.

"What are you doing?"

"Pleasuring you." He put his hand on her thigh and lightly dragged his thumb over the folds of her sex. "Is this where you touched yourself?"

"Yes." She moaned as he pressed more firmly.

"I'm going to touch you here too. I'm also going to put my mouth here." He looked up at her from between her legs. "Do you not want me to do that?"

She'd said she wanted everything, and she did. He'd told her she could do whatever she liked to him. She wanted him to do the same. "Do it. Please. I meant it when I said I wanted everything."

His answering smile was slow and wicked. "We won't be able to do everything today, but I look forward to our lifetime together when we will."

"I will imagine things you haven't yet experienced," she vowed.

"God, Cecilia, you are beyond anything I could have hoped for. I need to taste you *now*." He lowered his head to her sex and licked along her flesh.

Rapture flooded her, and she could feel the rush of ecstasy coming toward her, filling her, teasing her to that ultimate completion. Sliding one hand under her backside, he squeezed her flesh. Cecilia moved one leg to his shoulder, bending her knee slightly as he speared his tongue into her. His thumb massaged the top part of her sex, where she was most sensitive, and she bucked. He lifted his head slightly and his finger moved along her folds before slipping slowly into her. The sensation of him pushing inside her was exactly what she wanted. She clutched his head and moved her hips, desperate for more.

He sucked on that sensitive spot as he thrust into her and withdrew only to repeat the actions with greater speed. She felt as though she were rolling faster and faster down a steep hill, the world hurtling by as her body rejoiced in the speed and risk of coming apart when she reached the bottom. His tongue joined his finger, and he buried his face against her, his other hand stroking that delightful place until she couldn't hold on another moment. Her muscles clenched, and time seemed to still as unparalleled joy and pleasure flooded her. This was what she wanted. This was everything.

She seemed to float amongst the heavens as her body finished its convulsions. Belatedly, she realized that she'd likely horrified him with her wanton behavior. Except that he was the one who'd wanted to put his mouth there in the first place. And he clearly knew what he was doing.

Cecilia had thrown her arm over her eyes. Now she peeked out at him from beneath her wrist. "Did I embarrass myself?"

His hazel eyes glinted with heat. "I hope not. You were spectacular, in my opinion."

"So that was…normal?"

"I can't speak for anyone other than me, but that was exceptional."

"You've obviously done this before. You can say, objectively, I think, if I behaved horribly." She pressed her hand over her eyes, closing them.

She felt him move her arm.

"Open your eyes, Cecilia."

She did so, reluctantly.

He'd moved up over her, and his face was mere inches from hers. "Please don't feel shame for anything we do together in bed—or anywhere else we choose to engage in similar activities." He waggled his brows at her, then grew serious. "It doesn't matter if I've done this before because I haven't ever done it with *you*."

His words put her at ease and made her feel… good. He'd called her spectacular and said it was exceptional. What more proof did she need that she was not a wanton? Or that if she were, that was precisely what she should be?

She curled her hand around his neck. "I enjoyed that very much. Indeed, I feel quite satisfied."

His lips spread in a wide, masculine grin. "Excellent. I look forward to doing that with you again." He kissed her neck. "And again." He moved down to her breast once more, gently drawing on her nipple with his teeth.

"Was that your intent, then? To seduce me?" she teased. "Perhaps your scheme was to lure me to this cottage and make me yours."

He laughed, his body vibrating against hers. "Yes, I ensured there would be a terrible snowstorm." He kissed between her breasts and brought his head back up to hers. "You're the one who started the day with a scheme. I was merely hoping to endure our partnership and win the competition."

She shrugged as she wrapped her legs around him, opening her sex to feel his rigid cock against her. Closing her eyes briefly, she groaned softly. "I do think we won in the end." She looked at him, frowning slightly. "Though you have not. In fact, you haven't even removed your breeches." She rotated her hips against his. "I can feel that you need satisfaction."

"We don't have to."

"You said you were going to slide your cock into me. I demand that you do so."

He arched a brow at her. "Is that the kind of wife you're going to be?"

"The kind who asks for what she wants and expects her husband to deliver on his promises?" She reached between them and unbuttoned the fall of his breeches. "Absolutely."

"Then who am I to stand in your way? A happy wife is, I believe, the guarantee of a happy life."

Cecilia laughed as he jumped up and shed the remainder of his clothing. She sobered as soon as she saw the hard length of his cock. There was a moment's uncertainty as she considered how it would fit inside her, but she refused to be a silly nincompoop. Of course he would fit. And if his finger had been any indication, he would feel wonderful. The desire he'd so recently satisfied roared back.

"I want to be naked too." She sat up and unfastened one garter. He sat on the edge of the bed and loosed the other. Then he carefully rolled the stockings from her legs and set them on the floor.

"There," he said, raking her from head to foot with his hungry gaze. "Is that better?"

"It will be. As soon as you finish what you started."

He moved over her, sliding his legs between hers. "I am at your command."

～

*J*ohn could hardly believe his good fortune. He could so easily have been trapped in a snowstorm with a woman he didn't like or wasn't attracted to. Instead, he'd found Cecilia, someone he'd never expected to capture his attention and perhaps even his heart.

Looking into her eyes, he held his breath a moment. This woman was going to be his wife. Hopefully, the mother of his children. She would be at his side, and he would be at hers. He dipped his head and kissed her, softly, earnestly. Their bodies met, and she clasped his back.

The feel of her against him made his pulse quicken. He wanted so badly to make this good for her, and he planned to. In the years to come, they would look back on this and smile—he hoped.

She ran her hands down his back, then moved one between then. "May I touch you?" she whispered.

"Please."

"Of course. You said that I could. I just...I don't know what to do."

Bracing himself on his elbow, he brought his other hand to hers. "You can wrap your hand around it, if you like." He guided her hand to his cock, and she took him in her grasp.

"Like this?"

"Yes. It feels good if you stroke it. Move your hand up and down." He showed her, and she quickly found a stirring rhythm.

"Can you find your release doing this?" she asked.

"It requires faster movements." He demonstrated, guiding her hand more quickly along his shaft. "And faster still as the pleasure builds."

"Like you did with me—with your fingers and your mouth. Can I put my mouth on you there?"

"I *hope* you will, but not today."

"Why not today? Or tonight? You said we're probably going to be here until morning at least."

She made an excellent point, but he also didn't want to wear her out. "We'll see."

Her hand continued stroking him even as his grip slackened. "Do you do this to yourself?"

"Er, yes." He was having a hard time concentrating on what she was saying.

"I want to watch you sometime. Will you let me?"

That got his attention. John lifted his head and looked at her. "You are absolutely astonishing. Hell, yes, you can watch me." He envisioned an evening where they pleasured themselves together and nearly spent himself in her palm. "Enough."

He put his hand back over hers and guided his cock to her sex. "I'll go slowly." He'd never done this with someone for whom it was their first time. He hoped he wouldn't make a hash of it. "Lift your hips a bit."

She arched up, giving him a better angle. "Like this?"

"Just like that." He slid into her and groaned softly. She was so tight and hot around him. He stayed there inside her, letting their bodies acclimate to one another. "Is this all right?"

"It's very...full."

"Does it hurt? I understand it can hurt the first time."

"It's a trifle uncomfortable, but also pleasurable, which doesn't make a great deal of sense."

"I think I understand." He began to move very slowly. "How about now?"

"Oh! That is…nice."

Nice seemed underwhelming, but he would give it time. "Lift and wrap your legs around me, Cecilia."

She did so, her heels meeting his backside. "This is better." She gasped as he pushed back into her once more. "Faster, I think."

He didn't want to overwhelm her, but if that was what she wanted, he was more than happy to comply. A stray blonde hair teased her cheek. John brushed it aside and kissed her. "If at any moment you are uncomfortable, tell me to stop."

She nodded, then dug her feet into him. "Do not stop. I want to feel that release again."

He lifted his head, smiling. "Then let us find our climaxes together."

She met his thrusts eagerly, her hips moving in a delicious rhythm with his. She dug her fingers into his nape as he lowered his head to briefly capture her nipple in his mouth. A loud, delirious moan slid from her lips, and John gave himself over to the magic of their bodies working together.

His thrusts grew faster and deeper. Pleasure surged through him, guiding him to that blissful end. He wanted to share it with her, but he knew it might not be possible. Still, he would try. He straightened so he could access her sex with his hand. He teased her clitoris as he continued to drive into her.

Her muscles tightened, squeezing him. He moved his fingers faster and thrust deeper. She cried out his name, just as he'd hoped she would. He surrendered to the rapture rushing over him.

Just before he came, he pulled his cock from her body. Because he was late in his removal, he spilled himself on her thighs. Cursing, he gripped his shaft, finishing the job they'd started together and losing himself in the bliss of his orgasm.

When he came back to himself, John rolled to the side, careful not to fall off the narrow bed.

"Was that normal?" she asked.

He worked to regain the ability to speak, let alone explain. "It's not always that messy. I'm so sorry. I was preventing a baby. Or trying to, at least. I fear I was a little slow. Let me find something for you to tidy up."

Getting up from the bed, he glanced about the small cottage. They were woefully short on cleaning implements. He could give her his stock, but then he couldn't wear it tomorrow when they inevitably faced their parents, or whoever came in search of them.

She seemed to understand his consternation. "Just hand me my petticoat. I'll use an upper section."

He fetched the garment and handed it to her, turning his back to give her privacy.

"Why were you preventing a child?" she asked. "You're expected to produce an heir."

"Yes, but we needn't do so immediately. Your earlier comment about breeding gave me to think you weren't eager to be a mother."

"That is exceedingly thoughtful of you."

He turned then and was struck by the look of appreciation on her face. She seemed genuinely touched. And that made him want to kiss her again.

"I won't mind becoming a mother right away. I was being sarcastic earlier. Things have…changed since then." She let out a short, soft laugh.

"Indeed they have," he murmured.

"Come back to the bed," she said, setting her petticoat on the floor and turning onto her side so her back was to the fire. "I'm cold without you."

"You don't have to ask me twice." He got into the bed and faced her, drawing the coverlet over them. Then he wrapped his arms around her and drew her close. "Better?"

"Mmm, yes. We should use this as our defense. There was simply no other way for us to ward away the chill."

He fixed on the gold flecks at the center of her sherry-brown irises. "I don't think we'll need a defense."

"You think our parents are going to just pleasantly accept this situation?"

"It's not ideal, but it accomplishes their goal—we will be wed."

She stroked his shoulder. "And what of your goal? This is not what you planned. I'm sorry for causing us to get lost."

He put a finger over her lips. "We've been over this, and it's not your fault. I believe, in fact, that it was meant to be, that the universe righted a wrong done five years ago by bringing us together now."

Her lips curved into a sultry smile. "You think we were always supposed to fall in love and marry?"

Did that mean she was falling for him? Because he was already halfway gone for her. "I do. If you disagree, don't tell me."

She leaned forward, closing the small space between them, and kissed him. "As it happens, I think you're quite right."

CHAPTER 9

*W*as the house coming down? No, he was having a dream. No one would make that sort of racket.

John frowned as he blinked his eyes open. The moment he saw the low ceiling and felt the warm body against his, he recalled where he was. And with whom.

That noise had to be their rescuers pounding on the door.

"Open up!"

That was a man's voice, and not one John readily recognized. Was it her father?

He gently shook Cecilia. "My love, we are discovered."

Her eyes opened slowly, and they took a moment to focus. As soon as they did, they widened. "We were supposed to be awake and dressed!"

Yes, that had been their plan. The snow had stopped in the middle of the night, but there were several inches on the ground, at least in the clearing. John had presumed that anyone looking for them wouldn't be able to get to the cottage until late morning or even afternoon.

He'd been wrong.

"I shouldn't have underestimated a parent's urgency to find their missing child," he murmured.

John slipped from the bed, leaving the blanket that barely covered them to her. He pulled on his breeches and shirt as the pounding and shouting continued.

"Coming!" He gave Cecilia her chemise. "What do you want to do about your clothing?"

She grimaced. "It will take me far too long to dress before you answer them. But don't let anyone in. Tell them we'll come out in a bit."

He nodded, tucking his shirt into his breeches. He considered donning his stock and stockings, but that would only delay the inevitable. He smiled at her. "We've nothing to hide. This may not be the best circumstances, but the result will be what they wanted."

Feeling confident that all would be well, John went to the door and threw the bolt. Then he carefully opened the door and slipped outside.

His father and Cecilia's father stood together. Their host, Mr. Beverley, was off to the side, his features creased with concern. The fathers gaped at John, their eyes moving from his almost certainly disheveled hair to his underdressed form to his bare feet. Damn, it was cold, despite the sun coming out.

"What the devil are you about?" Lord Winchcombe, Cecilia's father, asked.

"I apologize for my dishabille," John said affably. "Our clothing was rather wet after we became trapped by the storm yesterday."

Cecilia's father's eyes bulged. "Good God, does Cecilia look like this? If you've ravished her—"

John held up his hand. "I believe the intention was for Cecilia and me to wed. We are most happily betrothed and look forward to the ceremony."

John's father, the Duke of Ironbridge, narrowed one eye at him, appearing skeptical. "You were not in favor of this just yesterday morning."

The baron snarled. "He's compromised my daughter and has no choice."

As anger began to stir within him, John fought to hold his temper. He had matured, but it seemed anything to do with Cecilia roused his passions. "The storm compromised us, I'm afraid. It hurried along our acquaintance, and our forced confinement led us to—quickly—determine that we do indeed suit."

"Harrumph. I want to speak with Cecilia."

"We will be out shortly," John said with a smile as he started to turn toward the door.

The baron put his hand on John's shoulder. "Dammit, she is my daughter. You will not manage her."

John turned a cool stare on his future father-in-law. "As she is soon to be my wife, I will advocate for her wishes, and her wish is that you remain here while we make ourselves presentable. There is no quarrel here, Winchcombe."

"This is a scandal! Everyone at the house party knows you are missing together." The baron glanced briefly toward Beverley.

"They know nothing," John said calmly. "Say that you found me in a tree and Cecilia in this cottage. Say we spent the night with tenants. You can fabricate whatever tale you like." He looked toward his father, hoping for his endorsement.

"John is right," the duke said. "This is our narrative to manage. We'll say they were found with one of the tenants and spent the night separately." He turned toward Beverley. "Can you support that story?"

Beverley nodded. "Of course. And since they will wed, the scandal would be minimal anyway."

Cecilia's father's face was bright red. "Still, I don't want it known that they were alone together in a tiny cottage overnight!"

"We five are the only ones who know that," John said.

"Six," Winchcombe interjected. "There's a coachman."

John nodded. "I have the utmost faith the tenant story is believable and will be expected. Indeed, it will be a romantic tale of how Cecilia and I fell in love under the watchful eye of a charming couple."

"Just so," Beverley agreed with a nod. "I know just the tenants who will happily go along with this. We will stop there on the way back to provide credibility to the story."

"A tale indeed," Winchcombe muttered.

"Brilliant." John smiled widely, ignoring his sour soon-to-be-father-in-law. "Now, if you'll excuse me." He turned to go back into the cottage, but his father snagged his elbow.

"A quick word, John," his father whispered.

They moved slightly away from the other men, but still under the watchful glower of John's soon-to-be father-in-law.

"You're certain this is what you want?" John's father asked, searching his face.

"It's what you wanted, isn't it?"

"Yes." His father exhaled. "However, when your child goes missing overnight—even when he is a grown man—things that seemed vitally important become less so. All the expectations I have for you as my heir are more about me than you. I know I've pushed you—in your studies, with your travels, to stand for a seat in the Commons, and now with marriage. In the end, I only want you to be happy."

John was speechless a moment. His father had always demanded excellence, but he'd never been harsh. "You sound regretful, and you needn't be. You are a good father, and what will make me happy is to follow your path. The first step is marrying a woman I think I may love."

A grin relaxed his father's features. "That is marvelous to hear. Don't let me keep you." He clapped John's shoulder.

With a nod, John turned and quickly slipped back into the cottage.

Cecilia had donned her corset and petticoat, and her stockinged feet peeked out from the hem. "I heard some of that. We spent the night with a tenant?"

John nodded as he sat on the bed to pull on his stockings. "Yes. I'm sorry to say that your father looks nearly apoplectic."

"That is not surprising. He despises even the hint of impropriety."

John pulled on his boots and plucked up his stock before standing. "This may have been an improper beginning, but if we hadn't been forced together, we might still be at odds."

Cecilia went to take her gown from the hook. "I'll tell him that."

They finished dressing, and John moved the bed back against the wall. He looked to Cecilia, who was trying to repair her hair. "Just put on your hat—it will cover the damage."

"Excellent point." She fetched the hat and set it atop her head, giving him a questioning look.

"Marvelous," he said, fetching her cloak and draping the outer garment over her shoulders.

She fastened the clasp at her throat. "Hopefully,

we will enter the house in such a way that we won't be seen."

"I'm sure your father will insist upon it," John said with a faint smile. He put on his hat and great-coat. "Ready?"

"I suppose. I admit I hate to leave our nest." She picked up the now-empty basket, for they'd eaten the contents last night.

John plucked up the bottle and tucked it into the basket before taking it from her. "Let me carry this."

"How gallant of you."

Moving to the door, he opened it while she stepped outside.

The three gentlemen had backed away from the door. Now, her father came forward. "Are you all right, Cecilia?"

"Never better, Father. I should think you are also quite pleased—you are gaining the son-in-law you wanted."

The baron frowned. "This is not the way it was supposed to come about."

"Nevertheless, this is what happened, and if it had not, I would likely still loathe Cosford. Instead, I find I am rather smitten. That's an excellent con-clusion, I think."

Her father appeared dubious. "This is not the conclusion, for you must wed."

"Of course they will," the duke said rather crossly. "Calm yourself, Winchcombe. We'll have the banns read as soon as we return to Ironbridge."

Cecilia's father sucked in a breath and threw back his shoulders. "Not Ironbridge. They will wed at St. Peter's in Winchcombe in four weeks' time, and they will have no contact until then."

John frowned. "Save the remainder of the house party." He flicked an uneasy glance toward his father, hoping he might advocate for them staying.

The duke gave John an almost imperceptible nod before addressing Winchcombe. "You can't mean to leave before it concludes day after tomorrow. That will only draw attention to...things."

"I suppose it would," the baron grumbled. "Fine. We will leave as scheduled. But then they won't see each other until the wedding."

Cecilia stepped toward her father. "Surely, we can spend some time together, especially over the holidays."

"No."

"Not even Epiphany?" she asked.

"I won't permit you to spend time with this blackguard until you are wed."

"He is not a blackguard, Papa," Cecilia said softly, sending an apologetic look toward John. "Without his aid, I might have frozen to death. Furthermore, if you think so poorly of him, why are you allowing the marriage at all?"

The baron's eyes glinted with fury. "It *must* happen, regardless of what anyone thinks or feels."

John supposed he could understand Winchcombe's anger, especially right now, having just discovered his daughter had spent the night with a man who wasn't—yet—her husband. However, he hoped the man's ire would resolve quickly.

"I think we can all agree that an unfortunate circumstance has turned out well," the duke said smoothly. "Come, let us be on our way. Beverley, you suggested a tenant who could provide an alibi?"

"Indeed, I know just the couple." Their host gestured to the coach. "After you."

Winchcombe moved to take Cecilia's arm before

John could. Then he guided her to the coach and sat her onto the forward-facing seat before settling in beside her. There would be no way for John to sit next to her, which was, of course, the baron's design.

John took the opposite seat along with his father, and Beverley squeezed in next to Winchcombe. John sent an encouraging nod toward Cecilia, but it didn't ease the furrows that had gathered on her brow. Later, he would smooth them.

Somehow.

❧

Following a short ride in the coach, they arrived at a charming cottage with a small collection of outbuildings that indicated it was a farm. Cecilia hadn't known what to expect, but was heartened by what she saw. This looked like a place where kind people resided.

Mr. Beverley, who'd talked the entire way from the woodcutter's cabin, perhaps to alleviate the awkwardness, left the coach and hurried toward the cottage to inform the residents of the proposed scheme.

"What will we do if they refuse to go along with this ruse?" Cecilia's father asked no one in particular.

Cecilia had felt his tension like a horrid chill as she'd been pressed against his side in the coach. "Might we get out?" she asked. The cool winter air would be preferable to the fraught atmosphere in the warmer space.

He cast her an irritated glance. "Not until we're sure there's a reason to."

Cecilia dared a look toward John. He was

glaring icicles at Cecilia's father. The frigidity of his glower comforted her. Already, he was an ally.

"I am confident the ruse will work," Ironbridge said amiably.

Cecilia was glad at least one of their fathers was behaving reasonably. "I am sure Mr. Beverley wouldn't have suggested it if he didn't share your confidence."

Their host returned to the coach wearing a broad grin. "Come inside. There's hot tea and warm bread."

A loud, embarrassing rumble sounded from Cecilia's middle. And was promptly echoed from John's abdomen. She stifled a smile, but he did not.

"That basket of food from yesterday was not enough to sate us, I'm afraid," John said.

"Then you must make haste!" Beverley held the door for them as Cecilia's father descended. After he helped her down, John and his father followed.

They made their way to the cottage, where they were immediately ushered inside. Rough-hewn beams stretched across the low ceiling of the main room, and a wide fireplace on the opposite wall crackled with a robust fire.

"Welcome," a woman in her midforties said. She smiled cheerfully, seeming to allow her attention to linger slightly on Cecilia. Was it because Cecilia wasn't removing her hat? She didn't dare, not with the unkempt state of her hair.

Mr. Beverley addressed everyone. "May I present His Grace, the Duke of Ironbridge, his son, Lord Cosford, Lord Winchcombe, and Miss Bromwell." He gestured to the woman and the man, who was of a similar age, standing beside her. "Allow me to present Mr. and Mrs. Harrison. They have been, ah, apprised of the situation and are eager to be of assistance."

"Indeed, we are." Mrs. Harrison moved toward Cecilia. "Would you like some tea, dear? Something to eat?"

"That would be lovely, thank you."

"Come to the table, then." Smiling gently, Mrs. Harrison guided Cecilia to the side of the main room, where a dining table was situated. Made of sturdy oak and adorned with a teapot and what smelled like a fresh loaf of bread, it was most inviting.

Cecilia slid into a chair and nearly leapt on the bread.

Blue eyes sparkling with kindness, Mrs. Harrison cut into the loaf and slathered a slice with butter before setting it on a plate and placing it in front of Cecilia. "I'll just pour your tea." Their hostess turned slightly. "Lord Cosford, you must join us."

A moment later, as Cecilia was already savoring her first bite of the delicious bread, John sat down beside her. He too was given a plate with buttered bread.

As he picked up his slice, he slid a look toward Cecilia. "Would it be in poor taste if I asked for jam?" he whispered.

She put her hand to her mouth as she worked to swallow around her laughter.

Mrs. Harrison set teacups near their plates. "There, now. Tuck in while I slice more bread, then I'll fetch some ham. Would you like eggs?"

"Yes, please," Cecilia said after barely swallowing.

"We won't have time for that," her father barked from behind her. He sounded as if he still stood near the doorway.

"Let them eat, Winchcombe," Ironbridge responded with considerable exasperation. "They're ravenous."

Cecilia could feel her father's scowl burning the back of her head. She really preferred to avoid his condemnation. "Perhaps we could just take a little with us in the coach," she suggested.

"Or we could stay here and eat," John said, throwing a glower of his own over his shoulder toward her father.

"I thought Miss Bromwell would also like to tidy up," Mrs. Harrison said.

Cecilia wondered what her hair looked like. "That *would* be nice."

"It's settled, then." The duke's voice boomed through the room. "They will eat and take a short respite to restore themselves." His tone was decisive. Still, Cecilia held her breath, waiting to hear if her father would argue.

Thankfully, he did not.

As John took another bite of bread, she leaned slightly toward him. "I can imagine your father brooked no quarrel in his house."

John kept his voice as low as she had. "Whenever he used that tone, you knew to close your mouth and keep it closed. And to vacate the room as soon as possible lest he become truly angry."

"I see." Cecilia sipped her tea, grateful for the warm brew.

A few minutes later, Mrs. Harrison brought ham and eggs. Cecilia devoured them with unlady-like haste. When she was finished, she gave John a sheepish look. "I promise, I don't usually eat like that. The quantity or the speed."

"Perhaps you didn't notice, but I wiped my plate clean when you still had a few bites left. You've no need to apologize." He chuckled softly. "I also don't typically inhale my repast."

Cecilia realized they had much to learn about each other. She shifted in her chair and finished her cup of tea.

"Ready to go upstairs?" Mrs. Harrison asked her.

"Yes, thank you."

John leapt up to hold her chair. Cecilia stood and quickly brushed her hand against his.

Mrs. Harrison looked to John. "Mr. Harrison is preparing a basin for you to wash up."

"I appreciate that most sincerely," he said, his gaze moving to Cecilia and staying there as she turned and accompanied Mrs. Harrison toward the staircase on the opposite side of the room.

They walked past the seating area near the hearth where the two fathers sat. The duke smiled at Cecilia, while her father frowned at the fire.

Part of her wanted to kick him. He was being ridiculous. Wasn't this the outcome he'd wanted? Hopefully, her mother would push him from his irritation.

Cecilia followed Mrs. Harrison up the stairs and into a bedchamber. "While you were eating, Mr. Harrison brought hot water up. It should be just the right temperature for you now. It's behind the screen there."

"Thank you," Cecilia said, grateful for the blessed woman's kindness. She moved behind the screen and nearly squealed with delight at the scent of lavender in the steam coming from the water. Mrs. Harrison had thought of everything.

"There's a mirror there as well as a hairbrush. I'm happy to help you redress your hair when you're finished."

"I think you must be an angel, Mrs. Harrison." Cecilia removed her hat and set it on the dresser next to the basin of water. Next, she unbuttoned her gown and scrubbed at her face and neck, feeling instantly refreshed.

"Hardly. I merely understand what it's like to be in a predicament and require the help of others."

"You have found yourself in a similar situation?" Cecilia asked.

"Indeed. When Mr. Harrison and I were first wed, we suffered a fire. We lost most of our belongings, and the structure had to be rebuilt. In the meantime, we had to live with neighbors, and during that period, I had my first child. Our kind hosts had five children of their own, so it was a busy time."

Cecilia could hear the smile in the woman's voice. "You sound as if you recall that fondly, but how can you? I'm so sorry that happened." Cecilia couldn't conceive of losing her home.

"It was incredibly upsetting, as you can well imagine, but I do have wonderful memories of the time we spent with our neighbors. They were so kind and generous. I vowed that I would always do what I could to help others."

Cecilia did the same right then—she would do whatever she could whenever she could to provide aid to those in need, whatever it may be. "Bless you, Mrs. Harrison." Finished washing, Cecilia rebuttoned her dress, then contemplated her reflection in the mirror. Her hair was a disaster. "I think I will need help with my hair, if you don't mind."

"Not at all. Should I come to you?"

"Yes, please." Cecilia removed the remaining pins from her hair.

Mrs. Harrison took one look at Cecilia's head and gave her a confident nod. "We'll set you to rights in no time." She pulled the chair away from the wall and gestured for Cecilia to sit. Then she fetched the brush and began to work at the knots in Cecilia's hair.

"What pretty blonde hair you have," Mrs. Harrison said. "Mine used to be this exact color."

"Isn't it still?" Cecilia resisted the urge to turn her head and look, but she was fairly certain the hue of the woman's hair matched her own.

"It's a bit paler. You can't see the white strands, but they're there. Mr. Harrison finds them attractive," she added with a mischievous lilt in her voice.

Cecilia smiled at that. "It sounds as though you and Mr. Harrison have had a happy marriage." She hoped for the same.

"Most definitely. I love him more today than yesterday and the day before that. He's been a wonderful partner—I've been lucky to have a husband who values me and treats me as someone he can rely on and consult."

She was indeed lucky. Cecilia grimaced as Mrs. Harrison worked the brush through a particularly tough knot. The woman murmured an apology, and Cecilia assured her all was well.

"How many children do you have?" Cecilia asked.

"Four. The older two are wed, and the younger two are out tending the sheep."

Again, Cecilia heard the joy in the woman's voice. Or the pride. Probably both. "Is this the life you envisioned for yourself? What you hoped for?"

Cecilia still hoped for love, but John had said he wasn't a romantic. He'd also said he thought they were meant to fall in love. Did that mean he loved her? She couldn't know until he said the words. Was she even ready to say the words herself?

"Absolutely," Mrs. Harrison said without pause. "The moment I met Mr. Harrison, I knew we were meant to share our lives. He wasn't struck with the same certainty, but it didn't take him long to come around." She laughed.

Cecilia couldn't resist turning her head to look at Mrs. Harrison as she set the hairbrush on the dresser. "What happened to change his mind?"

"Joseph Drucker took me for a ride in his cart. Mr. Harrison called on my father the very next day."

"Without speaking to you first?"

Mrs. Harrison began to pin Cecilia's hair up. "He told me he was certain in his feelings and in mine, even though I hadn't told him anything explicitly. He took a leap of faith, and he was right. We both were."

Cecilia couldn't help thinking of her own circumstances. She and John had taken a leap of faith last night. But what of their feelings and of...certainty? The necessity of marriage didn't allow for them to even consider their feelings.

Silence reigned as Mrs. Harrison finished Cecilia's hair. "I think that will suffice," she said finally. "Take a look and let me know if you agree."

Standing, Cecilia looked into the glass and smoothed her hand along the back of her upswept hair. The style was simple but elegant. Most importantly, it didn't look as if she'd spent the night in the arms of her lover.

Her *betrothed*.

"You are an angel and a magician," Cecilia said, turning to impulsively hug the woman. Indeed, she held on rather tightly.

"Goodness, you've had a difficult time, haven't you?" Mrs. Harrison patted her back. "Perhaps not difficult, but I imagine things have changed rather dramatically—and quickly."

Cecilia nodded as she pulled away. "What did Mr. Beverley tell you?"

"Only that you and his lordship were forced to spend the night together to get out of the storm and that you are newly betrothed."

"And he asked you to lie and say we were here."

"Which I am happy to do." Her brow puckered. "Unless you don't want me to? Am I mistaken in thinking you and his lordship are well matched? I thought I detected a distinct connection between the two of you."

"Did you?" Cecilia felt a giddy thrill amidst the anxiety swirling in her belly. At Mrs. Harrison's nod, Cecilia went on. "I confess I worry everything has happened so fast. At this time yesterday, I was plotting to ensure John and I would never see each other again. And now here we are, facing marriage. I'd hoped to marry for love and, well, we can't possibly be in love so soon, can we?"

"I think it's possible," Mrs. Harrison said slowly. "But only you can know that. And Lord Cosford, of course. I'm sure you will have time to determine your feelings for one another. From my perspective, you seem well on your way to a happy union." She smiled warmly at Cecilia.

Mrs. Harrison's words settled Cecilia's concerns. Things *had* happened quickly, and her father's grumpy demeanor wasn't helping matters.

"I do appreciate your help, Mrs. Harrison. I think John and I will be happy together."

And hopefully, love would come.

CHAPTER 10

$\mathcal{B}$y the time John climbed down from the coach when they arrived at Broadheath, Cecilia's father was already ushering her inside. It wasn't as if John had expected to kiss or otherwise touch her, but he'd hoped to at least exchange a few comforting words before they parted.

He was also eager to get some sense of how she was feeling. Their lives had completely changed overnight.

One spectacular, life-altering night in which he'd gone from wanting to get away from Cecilia at the earliest possible moment to desperate to spend the rest of his life in her company. It was an awesome—and, if he were honest, terrifying—revelation. Even so, he had no regrets as to how things had unfolded. But did she?

John hadn't seen her all day, not since they'd parted upon arriving. Now, as he made his way to the drawing room before dinner, he could only hope she would be present.

"John, wait just a moment."

Pausing outside the drawing room, John turned at the sound of his mother's voice. He'd already spoken to her when they'd returned that morning, and she was delighted to hear of his betrothal. However, she'd also seemed a trifle concerned.

Of average height with olive-green eyes and the warmest smile, the Duchess of Ironbridge never failed to put John at ease. Her mere presence added to his confidence and reassured him of his place in the world, in his family. He knew how blessed he was to have such a close bond with his parents and his siblings.

She gently touched his arm. "Were you informed about the plans regarding the betrothal announcement?"

"Only that Mr. Beverley would formally make the announcement this evening." John was fairly certain everyone at the house party already knew. His friends did, as each one of them had sought him out, and they'd gone to the billiards room to discuss the surprising turn of events.

John had carefully retold the details of their ruse of spending the night with the Harrisons. His friends had assumed the betrothal was simply a result of trying to avoid the appearance of impropriety and not due to any actual emotional—or physical—connection between John and Cecilia. He'd wanted to assure them most vociferously that they had connected on every level and there was nothing he wanted more than to wed her. However, he'd only said they'd found they would suit after all and were both amenable to the marriage. To say more would raise suspicion and invite further questions, both of which they needed to avoid.

The duchess nodded. "Yes, he'll do it before we remove to the dining room. You will escort Miss Bromwell, and the two of you will be seated together."

She would be present, then. John kept himself

from grinning. Despite that, it seemed he revealed himself somehow.

"This pleases you," his mother said with a chuckle.

"It's impossible to hide anything from you," John said with a sigh.

"You needn't hide that you've fallen in love with your bride—if that is indeed what has happened."

Love? To say that was what he felt seemed so premature, and yet John couldn't find another way to describe the joyous warmth and soaring anticipation that accompanied his every thought—all of which were centered on Cecilia.

John gave her what he hoped was a reassuring smile. "I believe I'll keep that between me and Cecilia."

His mother knew the truth about how they'd spent the night, but she hadn't pried for details. "Smart boy," she said. "I'll be speaking with her mother later about the wedding. You're sure the time and place are acceptable to you?"

Four weeks from now—on the sixteenth of January—in St. Peter's Church in Winchcombe. "Whatever is acceptable to my bride will be acceptable to me." John wanted to confirm that with Cecilia, since the time and place had been ordered by her father.

Smiling, the duchess gave him a light squeeze before removing her hand from his arm. "I hope Miss Bromwell knows what a wonderful man she is marrying. If not, given your brief association, I daresay she will very soon."

"Not if we aren't allowed to see one another," John said with a slight frown. Cecilia's father had reiterated before reaching Broadheath earlier that they would be kept apart until the wedding.

"Yes, well, I will speak with Lady Winchcombe

about that," John's mother said. "It's silly to keep you from deepening your acquaintance. You are betrothed, after all." She didn't state the obvious: that a betrothal was as good as being wed.

"I confess I don't understand his obstinance. Perhaps you'll have luck with his wife." John could only hope. In the meantime, he would make the most of tonight before the party ended tomorrow. He offered his mother his arm. "May I escort you into the drawing room?"

"Certainly." She smiled broadly and placed her hand on his sleeve.

Once inside, they spoke with Mrs. Beverley before parting. The duchess went to speak with another friend while John went directly to a footman holding a tray of wine. Selecting a glass of madeira, he took a hearty sip before he was accosted by Spetch.

The baron ushered John into the corner. "My wife has pleaded with me to find out the truth of what happened yesterday. And last night. You cannot leave me without sufficient information."

"Your wife should ask her friend." John had no doubt, however, that Cecilia would say nothing, just as he would.

Was that true? She'd promised her father that she wouldn't tell a soul the truth, but he couldn't say he knew her well enough to know if she meant it. Which wasn't to say he didn't trust her. He wouldn't have blamed her for wanting to talk with a friend. Wasn't that something women did? His sisters certainly did.

"Miss Bromwell has been closeted in her chambers all day. Dinah's efforts to see her have been rebuffed by Lady Winchcombe and Miss Bromwell's maid. Indeed, Dinah worries she won't even be in attendance tonight." Spetch lowered his voice. "She's concerned Miss Bromwell may have caught a chill and is actually ill."

A flash of distress sparked through John, but surely someone would have informed him if his betrothed had taken ill. No, this was her father—or both her parents—keeping her away from him. And her friends, apparently. John wished he could have words with his soon-to-be father-in-law, but his own father had counseled him against it, warning that Winchcombe might take any frustration he had with John out on his daughter. John did not wish to make things any more difficult for Cecilia.

"She is fine," John said evenly. "In fact, she will be here this evening."

"Dinah will be so relieved."

John scanned the room to see Lady Spetchley standing on the opposite side of the room with Main and his wife, Mrs. Mainwaring. He noted they all turned toward the doorway, their gazes fixed in unison. Turning, John saw the reason for their distraction.

Cecilia stood in the doorway on her father's arm, her mother on her other side. She still looked heart-stoppingly beautiful, her blonde curls arranged in an elegant style, her lush body draped in a gorgeous gown of blue shot with gold thread. He recalled every contour of her flesh, the taste of her lips and tongue, the sound of her pleasure.

And now he was growing hard. This would not do. He drank half his remaining madeira.

Though he wanted to go directly to her, he also didn't want to upset her father. He waited and watched as their hosts greeted Cecilia and her parents. Cecilia smiled briefly, but the sentiment didn't reach her eyes. At least not from John's perspective.

Hell, this was torture, standing so far away from her and trying to guess at her disposition. He took a drink of wine and set the not-quite-empty glass on a table before striding toward the doorway.

Mr. Beverley saw John approach and gave him a nod. "And here's the groom. Seems like now would be a good time to make the announcement?" Beverley looked toward Winchcombe, which grated on John's already fraying nerves.

"Indeed, it would," John said quickly before Winchcombe could respond. Next, John reached for Cecilia's hand and bent over it before brushing his lips against her glove. "Good evening, Cecilia. You are lovelier than ever." He felt a tremor along her hand and quashed a smile.

"Thank you," she murmured.

"Come," Beverley gestured toward them and moved toward the center of the room.

John gave Cecilia his arm and ignored Winchcombe's glower. He caught Lady Winchcombe whispering to her husband that he oughtn't look as if he were not in favor of their marriage. The baron twisted his expression into one of impassivity. John supposed that was better than irritation.

"I hope you've passed a reasonably tolerable day," John said softly as they accompanied their host.

"Reasonably tolerable is...generous. My mother confined me to bed to ensure I hadn't caught a cold." Cecilia rolled her eyes. "I am and have been fine."

John was relieved to hear it. He glanced toward Winchcombe. "Your father's mood doesn't appear to have improved."

"No, it does not. His anger typically takes time to cool."

Alas, there was no more time for discussion as Beverley announced their betrothal as well as his glee that the match had been made at his house party. This was followed by a line of people congratulating them, then they progressed into the dining room.

While John was seated next to Cecilia, they were not able to privately converse. He did ascertain that she was well.

As the final course was drawing to a close, John leaned toward Cecilia. "I'll excuse myself from the dining room in a quarter hour. Meet me in the small sitting room next to the library."

Cecilia's brown eyes rounded briefly, and she looked as if she would protest. John put his hand on hers beneath the table.

"Just try," he murmured. Then he stood and helped her from her chair, and the women departed the dining room.

John spent the next quarter hour trying not to glower at Cecilia's father. Eyeing the clock on the mantel, he grew more anxious as each minute passed.

"Everything all right?" Main asked. He'd moved to take Cecilia's chair while the port was poured, and Spetch had taken the chair to John's left. Their other friend, Priest, was on the other side of Main.

"Impeccable," John said as he picked up his glass. He finished the last of his port, realizing he'd imbibed his at a much faster rate than anyone else. It wasn't quite the appointed time, but John couldn't stand another moment of waiting. "Pardon me," he murmured. "I'll be back shortly."

Some men relieved themselves behind a screen in the corner of the dining room that was placed after the ladies had gone, but John had never taken to that practice. Regardless, that wasn't the purpose for his departure.

Once he left the dining room, John walked quickly to the sitting room, hoping that Cecilia might already be waiting for him. She was not. He forced himself to lean against the wall next to the door so that he was not easily visible inside the room in case anyone happened by.

It was another ten minutes until he heard the whisper of skirts and the tap of heels. His heart beat faster as he anticipated her entrance.

Then she was there, moving over the threshold. John curled his arm around her and drew her out of the way so he could close the door softly but firmly. His eyes met hers just before he lowered his head and claimed her mouth, kissing her as he'd longed to do since they'd been interrupted that morning. It was hard to believe it hadn't even been a day since he'd held her in his arms—it felt like it had been forever.

She wrapped her arms around his neck and returned his kiss, their tongues clashing as he pressed her against the door. His body raged with desire, and he wondered if they ought to take a risk...

Tugging at his hair, she broke the kiss and looked up at him. "We will be leaving first thing tomorrow, and then I'm not to see you until the wedding."

"Blast," John breathed. "My mother plans to speak with your mother about that. We'll find a way."

Cecilia frowned. "My father can be incredibly obstinate."

He stroked his knuckles along her cheekbone. "How will I navigate the next month without seeing you? Without touching you? Without holding you in my arms? I want nothing more than to spend every moment with you so that I may know you entirely—body and soul."

She shivered beneath his touch. "This is all so… overwhelming. A day ago, I believed I'd come up with a way to ensure I wouldn't ever have to see you again. Now, you are to be my husband."

"I had the same thought." He hoped she'd also come to the same conclusion he had. "But I have no regrets as to what happened. It is not the courtship I envisioned with my bride, but the result will be just as sweet."

"You sound so certain."

"I am." John wished he could find a way to reassure her that all would be well. He cupped her face and looked into her eyes. "I have no doubts whatsoever. Yesterday, we were delivered into each other's arms, and I believe with every fiber of my being that this was meant to be. That *we* were meant to be."

He knew in that moment that he *did* love her. Shockingly. Unbelievably. Miraculously.

But he didn't tell her so for fear that he would only compound a situation that had happened at lightning speed. "What can I do to help you feel less overwhelmed?" he asked.

She shook her head, and he lowered his hands. "I don't know. I'm sure it's partly due to my father. He's just so grumpy."

"Perhaps you can just ignore him?" John asked. He lifted her hand and pressed a kiss to the back.

"I can try, but my mother says that he thinks you lured me to the woodcutter's cottage and seduced me." Cecilia averted her gaze. "My mother asked me several times if I truly wanted this marriage or if I'd been manipulated into it."

"And you told her you had not." John held his breath waiting for her answer.

"Of course. Perhaps I just need to convince my father, and he'll become more agreeable. Hopefully then he will allow us to see one another."

John considered whether he ought to speak with her father. There'd been no manipulation, save Mother Nature ensuring he and Cecilia had the opportunity to realize they would suit. "I will hope for that too." He leaned toward her for another kiss.

Before he could press his lips to hers, she stepped from his embrace, giving him an apologetic look. "I need to return to the drawing room before I am missed."

Then she was gone.

John would bloody well make sure her father knew this was a union they both wanted, that John cared deeply for Cecilia. That he loved her.

Perhaps that was what Winchcombe needed to hear.

But John would be damned if he didn't tell Cecilia first.

CHAPTER 11

*A*s Cecilia finished preparing for bed that night, her mother came into her chamber. Cecilia's maid, Ferris, retreated to the small dressing room where her pallet was located, and Cecilia stood rigid next to the edge of her bed.

"Tonight went very well," the baroness said as she went to perch on a chair set against the wall opposite Cecilia's bed.

Cecilia eyed her mother, who was still garbed in her evening wear. While Cecilia had retired relatively early—primarily to avoid her father's glower—she imagined many people were still downstairs enjoying the final night of the party.

When Cecilia said nothing in response, her mother continued, "I had a nice conversation with your soon-to-be mother-in-law. She is most eager to welcome you into their family."

Because Cecilia had also spoken with John's mother, she already knew this. It also made her keenly aware of how she was being made to feel as if she'd done something wrong, while John's family was more than pleased with how things had turned out. Frustration with her parents kept Cecilia's mouth sealed.

"Did you enjoy dinner with your betrothed?"

"As much as I could." Cecilia focused her gaze on one of the posts of her bed rather than on her mother.

The baroness exhaled. "I don't know why you are upset."

"Of course you don't. You and Papa see nothing wrong with acting as though I've committed a great transgression. I didn't plan to be stranded with Cosford." Cecilia was careful to use John's title lest her parents think her use of his first name was proof of her looseness.

"I know you didn't," her mother said softly. "I do apologize for how this has all happened. It has not been...ideal."

Cecilia looked to her mother. "No, it has not. However, the result is what you wanted, so why not be happy instead of agitated about a scandal that isn't going to happen? Even if it did, why should we concern ourselves? I will be a duchess someday."

"Duchesses are not impervious to scandal." The baroness pursed her lips. "I do think we have avoided such scandal, however. If anyone discusses the events of yesterday, there may be speculation, but we can't control that."

"People who enjoy gossip and pushing others down will speculate regardless of the circumstances. At some point, you have to hold your head up and ignore commentary, Mama."

"While that is true, if people are aware of what actually happened—"

"No one, save John and I, knows what actually happened." This time, Cecilia used his name on purpose. Clearly, her mother was going to think what she wanted. "And no one ever will."

"Come now, you won't tell your friends? Of

course you will, and one of them may spill your secrets."

Cecilia knew they would not, but she wasn't going to argue the point with her mother. "I haven't told a soul, and I won't—including you." The baroness had tried to pry details from Cecilia, but she'd confessed nothing beyond saying she and John had determined they would suit, and for that, her mother should be grateful. Nothing else mattered—at least to them.

"I understand. And I shan't press you any further." Her mother did sound apologetic, which mollified Cecilia—slightly. "I just pray this is the match you want. I was trying to ensure you would marry for love. I hope you know that." She met Cecilia's gaze, and the sincerity nearly made Cecilia share her worry.

What if John didn't come to love her?

Why was she thinking such things? He might not be a romantic, but he'd thought they were destined to fall in love. Surely that meant he was already on his way? "I would have preferred a courtship," Cecilia admitted.

"Circumstances have prevented that," Cecilia's mother said. "At least you no longer loathe him."

"I do not," Cecilia agreed, thinking that she might, in fact, love him.

"I believe this will turn out well," the baroness added with surprising certainty. "You will see. Our family has a history of successful matchmaking, all the way back to Queen Elizabeth's court."

Cecilia was aware of their family's history. An ancestor had been a formal matchmaker in the queen's court. Ever since, women in their family had taken the occupation of matchmaking, whether it was wanted or not, very seriously. "Is it really true that none of the marriages arranged by our family have been failures?"

"That is the legend."

Her use of the word "legend" did not inspire confidence, but Cecilia would not base her relationship with John on "legends." She put her hand to her mouth as if she were yawning. "You must excuse me, for I am rather tired."

She was not, actually, since her mother had forced her to stay in her chamber all afternoon. Cecilia had napped, which hadn't been difficult due to not getting a full night's sleep. How she wished she could go back to the cozy intimacy of the woodcutter's cottage with John.

The baroness stood. Cecilia didn't move from the side of the bed.

"Good night, my dear. I will endeavor to arrange for a private moment between you and Lord Cosford before we depart tomorrow." She gave Cecilia what was supposed to be a reassuring smile. Except, Cecilia had grave doubts as to her mother's success. Papa was incredibly stubborn.

"Thank you." Cecilia crossed her arms over her chest in case the baroness decided to try to initiate a hug.

With a nod, Cecilia's mother left.

Cecilia blew out a breath. Then she stared at her bed and wondered how she was ever going to sleep. Having spent last night in John's arms, she didn't want to be alone. She also wanted the comfort of his reassurance that all would be well, that he desired a loving marriage as much as she did, and that the next month would pass quickly.

∽

*S*omehow, Cecilia had managed to fall asleep, which she knew because she was now being awakened. A hand gently shook her shoulder.

"Cecilia?"

She opened her eyes, but the room was still dark. Still, she recognized the voice. "John?"

"Shh. Will you come with me?"

Pushing the coverlet off, Cecilia sat up. "Where?"

"Just come with me," he whispered, taking her hand.

"What about my dressing gown or my slippers?"

"You don't really need them, but I'll wait if you want them."

"What if we're caught?" Cecilia shook her head. "My father would be apoplectic."

"We won't be. We're only going a short distance. Will you trust me?"

She squeezed his hand. "I trust you."

"I never knew those three words could be so arousing," he murmured before kissing her hard and fast.

Cecilia's body thrilled. The connection between them certainly hadn't waned since last night. She realized in that moment that she would risk anything to be with him, even her father's ire.

He pulled her from the bedchamber and a short distance along the corridor. Then he opened a barely visible door in the paneling—it had a painting on the front of it—and tugged her inside. "I found this well-placed cupboard and thought it would be a better place to be with you in the middle of the night than your bedchamber. I recalled you mentioned your maid is ensconced in there with you." He spoke in a slightly louder tone than before, but still kept his voice low.

"Yes, she sleeps on a pallet in the dressing room." The cupboard was even darker than her bedchamber since there wasn't a fireplace to provide even meager light from dying embers. "I wish I could see you. Why did you bring me here?"

"I couldn't bear to say goodbye to you tomorrow without holding you one more time. Is that all right?" He sounded uncertain.

"It's more than all right." She curled her hands around his neck and pulled him down to kiss her. Their lips met, and he immediately groaned. Then his tongue drove into her mouth, and she was overcome with a desperate need to feel him against her. Their kisses were torrid and frantic, as though they couldn't get enough. At least, that was how Cecilia felt. Between kisses, she said, "I confess I would prefer a bed to a cupboard."

"As would I." He kissed her neck, his lips and tongue arousing her to a fevered height.

She pushed at him. "I can't take anymore."

He caressed her cheek. "My sweet Cecilia. I want you so badly. I could take you here. If you'll allow it."

"Standing?" Cecilia's body throbbed with want. "Yes. Please. Now."

"Lift your night rail to your waist," he rasped just before his hand dove into the neckline of the garment and cupped her breast.

Cecilia moaned as he tweaked her nipple, massaging and squeezing her. She managed to tug up her night rail to her waist. He pressed against her, the heat of his flesh meeting hers. Gasping, she clutched at his shoulder with her free hand.

He clasped her hip as he pushed her firmly against the back of the cupboard. Then he lifted her leg and curled it around his waist. "Keep that there." He kissed her again while his hand moved over her thigh, and his fingers stroked along her sex. Rubbing her flesh, he created a delicious friction. She whimpered into his mouth, desperate for her release.

"Come for me, Cecilia. I can feel you're close. Come for me before I put myself inside you. I want to feel your tremors around my cock." He circled the top of her sex, then slid his finger into her sheath.

She cried out against his mouth as her muscles clenched. Then he was pushing inside her, filling her and sending her deeper into the dark ecstasy of her release.

His hands cupped her backside. "Put your other leg around me. I've got you."

Cecilia wrapped herself around his waist, locking her ankles behind him. He groaned as he drove into her, his lips claiming hers once more.

Her release continued until it somehow became another desperate climb for gratification once more. He filled her over and over, sending her into a mindless frenzy of desire. His mouth left hers, and he kissed her ear. "I love you, Cecilia. Now and forever."

She heard his words, but she was too far gone to respond or to even really understand what he was saying. Digging her heels into him, she came again, trying desperately to keep her moans and whimpers from leaving their small, enclosed space.

He started to pull away from her, and she knew he meant to prevent a baby. She didn't care about that. They were to be married, and she wanted to be a mother. Most importantly, she didn't want him to leave her.

"Don't go," she said, holding him tightly against

her. At some point, she'd abandoned her grip on her night rail, not that it mattered.

"You're sure?" he asked, sounding strained.

"We're to be married. Of course I'm sure."

Still, he pulled out of her and set her down.

"John, you didn't have to do that."

"A moment," he bit out.

She knew he had to finish and didn't want him to do it alone. Finding him in the darkness, she curled her hand around his. "Let me." Then she dropped to her knees and took him in her mouth.

"*Cecilia.*" He clasped her head as she followed her instincts, using her mouth and tongue to pleasure him. "You can't."

She gripped his hip, digging her fingers into him as answer as she worked her mouth around him, swallowing him as deep as she could. He pumped into her, his movements growing more frantic until he again tried to pull away. "Don't," she managed as she held him even tighter.

"I'm going to spill in your mouth."

With her other hand, she cupped his balls, again using her instinct, hoping that her wordless reply told him exactly what she wanted. His cock brushed the roof of her mouth as he came. She swallowed her surprise along with his seed. When he was finished, she rose, her body still quivering with satisfaction.

"Cecilia, you astonish me," he said softly before taking her in his arms and brushing his lips over hers.

She pulled back, wishing again that she could see him. "Did you say you loved me?" She had to have imagined that.

"I did. But please don't feel you have to say it back—not unless you're sure."

"And you are?" Cecilia shook her head. He

wouldn't lie. Of that she was certain. "I love you too."

"If you could only see my smile. I fear my face may break." He laughed softly.

"Oh, John." Cecilia kissed him again. "I wish we didn't have to be apart for so long."

"I am going to do everything in my power to make sure we aren't. Now, let's get you back to your chamber."

He opened the door to the cupboard and escorted her into the dimly lit corridor. A moment later, he ushered her into her bedchamber.

"Good night, Cecilia. Sleep well. I know I will." He gave her a disarming grin, probably just like the one she hadn't been able to see in the cupboard, before departing.

They loved each other. This was real. This was the marriage she'd dreamed of.

If only her father weren't being so difficult. It wasn't fair, not when this was what he'd wanted.

While Cecilia appreciated John's commitment to ensuring they would not be apart, she needed to speak with her father. She wouldn't allow him to come between her and the man she loved.

CHAPTER 12

*J*ohn woke feeling a mixture of bliss and dread. His joy at recognizing and sharing his love with Cecilia was immeasurable. Hearing that she loved him too had somehow made him feel even more buoyant. This was pure joy. And he wasn't going to suffer a month away from her.

Determined, John went down to the dining room for breakfast. He was early and anticipated he might even be the first to arrive.

He was wrong. Winchcombe was already there and looked up sharply as John entered.

"Morning, Winchcombe," John said cheerily, intent on keeping the baron from provoking him.

"You're up early, Cosford." Wincombe went back to his plate of food.

"I typically am." John went to the sideboard and helped himself to a variety of items before taking the chair next to Winchcombe at the table.

The baron slid him a narrow glance that seemed to ask why John was sitting *there*.

"I appreciate a little time to get to know you better since Cecilia's and my courtship has been so, er, brief." John used his most amiable tone.

"It was nonexistent," Winchcombe grumped.

"Which is why it would be wonderful if we could all spend the next month deepening our acquaintance."

"You can't cry off. We'd sue for breach of promise."

"I've no intention of crying off. I love your daughter and am wholly committed to her and our life together."

"Stuff and nonsense," the baron said, surprising John with his reaction. "You can't love her, so don't think you can lie to me."

John set his utensils down and angled himself toward Winchcombe. "Why can't I love her?"

"After one night? Her mother tells me she loathed you before, that she was not at all interested in a match with you. And I'm to believe she's suddenly eager to wed you?" Winchcombe snorted. "I am not a fool."

Trying to see this man's perspective, John imagined how he might feel if his daughter had expressed her preference to not wed a man, only to be trapped with him overnight so that their marriage was forced. "I can only think how this looks to you," he said quietly. "However, the best possible result happened from the unfortunate circumstance of Cecilia and me being stranded together. We found we not only suited, but that we are perfectly matched. I love her beyond reason, and I realize how that must sound to you." He wouldn't speak for Cecilia, though he knew she loved him too.

"It's true, Papa." Cecilia stepped into the dining room, surprising John—and apparently her father, as they both snapped their heads in her direction and leapt to their feet. "I love John, and I am grateful we had the chance to get past our initial...misgivings."

John tamped down his smile, which was no easy feat given the way Cecilia's lush mouth was twitching with mirth. Misgivings, indeed.

"I don't see how you can know you're in love," Winchcombe said gruffly.

"Just because I made you wait an interminable three months before I would accept your proposal so I could make sure we were in love doesn't mean they can't know." This came from Lady Winchcombe, who'd entered behind her daughter, and now Cecilia's head was snapping toward her along with John's and the baron's.

"You never told me that," Cecilia said.

The baroness shrugged. "It didn't signify. Anyway, everyone is different. Your father and I did not share an instant connection. Perhaps we should have tried becoming stranded alone together."

Cecilia put her hand to her mouth, but John could see that she was trying not to laugh. "John and I did not share an instant connection either. Actually, we did. Instant mutual loathing."

"That sounds about right." John couldn't keep from grinning.

"Which is why I find this falling in love nonsense so unbelievable! I know how badly Cecilia wants to marry for love, but this situation requires she marry this man." Winchcombe looked to his daughter. "I hated the idea that you were being forced into something you didn't want, even while knowing you had no choice."

"Papa, if I still couldn't abide John, would you really have made me marry him?" Cecilia asked softly.

The baron looked down at his plate. "No. But it

would have caused an irreparable scandal." He returned his gaze to Cecilia. "I wouldn't have wanted you to endure that either. Is it wrong for me to want you to be free of turmoil?"

Cecilia smiled at him. "No, it's not. It's quite lovely, actually. I just wish you'd told me that."

John agreed with everything she said. He was also glad to hear her father's behavior had been driven by care for his daughter.

"Does this mean you're ready to accept that you can't keep them apart until the wedding?" the baroness asked with a crisp tone. The corner of her mouth ticked up in a half smile. "I need to get started on planning the betrothal ball for Epiphany."

A ball? Brilliant. But then John would have taken any excuse to see Cecilia. Still, Epiphany was some way off. He didn't want to celebrate even one Christmas without Cecilia. "Since we will spend Epiphany at Isbourne Hall and the wedding will be just ten days later in Winchcombe, might I suggest you join us for Christmas at Ironbridge?" John was certain his parents wouldn't mind.

Lady Winchcombe wrinkled her nose briefly as she made her way to the sideboard. "That is most kind of you, but I do prefer to spend Christmas at Isbourne Hall. I'll also need to be there planning the ball."

"Then perhaps Cecilia can come. She will be well chaperoned." John wished his parents were present to support him.

As if conjured by his thoughts, his parents came into the dining room. "Good morning," the duke said with a hearty smile. "Just the people I was hoping to break my fast with."

John looked to his father. "We were just discussing a betrothal ball that Lord and Lady Winch-combe will host on Epiphany at Isbourne Hall."

John's mother brightened. "How splendid! What a wonderful way to spend the holiday."

"I couldn't agree more," John said. "And though Lord and Lady Winchcombe need to remain at Is-bourne Hall for Christmas, I've invited Cecilia to join us at Ironbridge."

The duchess smiled at Cecilia. "Oh, that would be lovely. I do hope you can come."

"I'd like that," Cecilia said. "I'm sure my Great-Aunt Susan would be delighted to accompany me as my chaperone." She glanced toward her mother, who'd filled her plate and moved to the dining table.

Though John had no idea who Great-Aunt Susan was, he was already devoted to her.

Cecilia helped herself to breakfast along with John's mother and father, then she joined him at the table. John pulled back the chair next to his in invitation. She set her plate down and took the of-fered seat.

"Coffee or tea?" John asked, intending to pour for her from the pots on the table.

"Tea, thank you."

"All right, you may spend Christmas at Iron-bridge." It wasn't the baron's booming proclama-tion that startled John, but what he'd said. Having just picked up the teapot, John fumbled, and hot brown liquid steamed over the tablecloth and onto Cecilia's plate.

John gasped and nearly dropped the teapot. He managed to set it down abruptly before he caused further damage. He swept up his napkin. "Are you all right? Did I scald you?"

"Fortunately, the tea did not reach me," Cecilia said, sounding amused. "Has anyone ever told you that you're a menace, particularly when it comes to beverages?"

His lips twitched. "In fact, they have. And they were not wrong."

Cecilia's eyes twinkled with mirth. "I hereby forbid you to wield a beverage within two feet of me." She moved away from the table as a footman tidied the mess.

John's mother looked to Cecilia and John. "I was going to suggest that you should both remove to the breakfast room so you can dine in relative privacy before we depart."

"Capital idea," John said, ready to grab his plate. Or not. He could think of a dozen other things he'd rather do with Cecilia than eat. Though he supposed one of those things involved his mouth tasting her...

"We must all remove to the breakfast room," Winchcombe said. "This table needs to be remade."

"I'll just move your plates to the breakfast room," a footman offered. He brought a tray and collected the items on the table before hastening from the dining room.

"We'll meet you there," John's father said. "Then we can discuss the specifics of Cecilia's journey to Ironbridge and the betrothal ball."

A few moments later, the duke winked at John before departing the dining room and leaving John and Cecilia alone with the footman and a maid who'd arrived to clean the table.

Cecilia grabbed John's hand and tugged him from the room. "Where can we go? Do you know of a cupboard nearby?"

"I do not," John said with a grin. "But we should probably go to the breakfast room. We've just won major victories. We oughtn't try our luck."

"Wait just a moment." Cecilia let go of his hand, and he turned to face her.

He noted the crease in her brow. "Is something wrong? I thought you'd be pleased with the turn of events."

"I definitely am. It's just... Why did you leave me last night when I said you didn't have to?"

He froze a moment as he worked to collect his thoughts. "I, ah, I didn't want you to feel trapped. Again."

She blinked. "I don't feel trapped. Do you?"

"Not at all. But I don't think either of us can deny that we did in those first moments in the woodcutter's cottage. Am I wrong?"

"No." A smile curled her lips.

"My love, I would choose you a thousand times." He shook his head. "Always. I would *always* choose you."

"When I told you not to leave, I meant it—that was my choice. Unless...would you rather not have children right away?"

He hadn't really considered it, which was foolish. He'd been too focused on how completely his life had changed. "I don't know. I do know that I want time with you. So perhaps I would prefer to wait." If that were even possible. He knew the prevention of a child was shoddy work at best.

"We should have discussed it instead of relying on our wits while we were in a fit of passion."

John laughed again. "You make an excellent point." He sobered, looking her in her eye. "I apologize for not listening to you. Your wishes, your *choices*, are very important to me. Please tell me you would choose to come to Christmas at Ironbridge, that I didn't create an awkward situation in which you felt you had to say yes?"

"Never fear, my love, I want nothing more than

to spend this Christmas with you, wherever that may be, and every Christmas thereafter."

He swept her in his arms and kissed her soundly. With great reluctance, he pulled away. "We need to get to the breakfast room. I'm most eager to determine when you can travel to Ironbridge for Christmas."

She looped her arm through his. "As quickly as possible."

EPILOGUE

*N*ear the end of the wedding breakfast, John sidled close to his wife. "When do you think everyone will leave? I'm quite desperate to be on our way." They would depart for Blickton, the ancestral home of the earls of Cosford. Now it would be their home.

"So you can ravish me in the coach?" Cecilia asked with a laugh.

He waggled his brows at her. "This time, we will not be chaperoned." They'd traveled with his parents to see it when Cecilia had visited Iron-bridge at Christmas.

"And here I was looking forward to an actual bed. I thought we were finally past meeting behind damp hedgerows and in tight alcoves. Or jostling coaches."

"Don't forget cupboards. And the cowshed." John had found the cowshed interval last week particularly delightful.

"Your impulsivity knows no bounds."

He laughed. "You knew that about me years ago. And I do have some restraint, else I would have carted you off an hour ago."

"People have already begun to depart," Cecilia said. "It won't be long now."

"I promise to keep my hands to myself until we arrive at the inn." It would take two days to reach Blickton.

She gave him a saucy smile. "I think we can find ways to build our anticipation, at least."

John groaned as desire roared through him. "You will torture me, wife."

"All the rest of your days." She smoothed her features. "Furthermore, I do not want to make a mess in the coach." She was referring to the fact that John always finished outside her in an effort to prevent a baby. They'd decided they preferred to wait—at least a year—in order to enjoy one another as they started their life together.

John nodded in agreement. "I suppose that is a wise decision."

Their friends, Spetch and his wife, Dinah, joined them.

"Time for us to be on our way," Spetch said. "I'm due back in London tomorrow."

Cecilia smiled at him and Dinah. "We do appreciate you sharing our day with us."

"We would never have missed it," Dinah vowed. "I'm still amazed that you two are married, let alone madly in love."

"I would not have put a wager on it," Cecilia said with a laugh.

"Will you be hosting any entertainments at Blickton?" Spetch asked. "It's a wonderful estate. I'd love for Dinah to see it."

Cecilia nodded. "Of course we will. You should plan on a house party in the autumn. I do love a good house party and look forward to hosting our own."

"We'll see where we are with the refurbishments we discussed," John said. They'd made plans to redecorate several rooms, and eventually, he wanted to enlarge the orangery.

"Oh, it will be fine." Cecilia breezily waved her hand.

"Why not have the party in the summer?" Spetch suggested. "Then we could take boats out on the lake."

Cecilia narrowed her eyes at him. "If you think I'm going to host a house party with boats, you have a very short memory."

Spetch laughed, and John joined him.

"Actually, the lake isn't deep enough in the summer for boats," John said. "We could go out in the autumn, but if someone fell in, it would be quite cold."

Dinah shook her head. "No, thank you. Since I know that's a distinct possibility, I'll skip it."

"Fair enough," Spetch said.

They said their goodbyes, and soon it was time for John and Cecilia to depart. Her mother embraced her tightly. "I'm just so glad you are happy," she said to her daughter.

"I am, Mama. More than I ever dreamed." Cecilia hugged her father next.

The baron stepped back with a gruff cough. "I am also pleased. Your happiness is all I ever wanted."

"Thank you, Papa. You and Mama chose a wonderful husband for me." She slid a love-filled look toward John who felt as though his heart might burst.

John's parents were also ready to depart and said their goodbyes to Lord and Lady Winchcombe. They were traveling in the same direction as John and Cecilia, but they would not be riding in the same coach. Indeed, though they would spend tonight in the same town, John's father had made a point of reserving lodging at a different inn from John and Cecilia. He'd insisted the bride and groom required privacy. John had never appreciated his father more.

John hugged him extra tightly before they separated to climb into their coaches. "Thank you for your support through this entire betrothal."

"You shall have it always. I couldn't be more delighted to welcome Cecilia into her family. She is already an excellent countess. I look forward to seeing what comes next." The duke's eyes glinted with mirth. "Your mother would like a grandchild."

Chuckling, John opened the door of his father's coach. "Yes, well, we'll see what happens."

His mother was already inside, and John quickly clasped her hand. Then he hurried to join Cecilia.

"Ready?" he asked.

She snuggled against him and pulled a blanket over their laps. "More than."

~

*U*pon arriving at the inn, John had indeed swept his bride up to their suite. While he'd enjoyed all their encounters over the past month, there was something sweet about sharing a bed with his wife.

"Was that worth the wait?" he asked as she snuggled against him.

Cecilia snorted. "We hardly waited. Shall I count the number of times we've been together since the house party?"

"I meant the coach ride," John said with a laugh.

"Oh, yes, definitely that. But it's the bed that I'm

appreciating the most. That aspect is more than welcome."

"Hmm, as usual, you make a brilliant observation. It's hard to believe we haven't been in a bed together since the snowstorm."

"I was so upset that day. Not only had my plans utterly failed, I'd been delivered into the hands of the menace."

"And I'd been saddled with a shrew—not just for an evening, but a lifetime."

Cecilia rolled over on top of him and straddled his hips. "Saddled like this, you mean?"

John's gaze went to her magnificent breasts. "This was not even a distant thought at that moment," he managed to say. He was growing hard again, and here he thought they might have dinner soon. Food could wait. He found he was absolutely ravenous—again—for his wife.

"And now?"

John put both his hands on her breasts, cupping and massaging them. "I am consumed with thoughts of you."

Her eyes slitted as he pulled on her nipples. "Do you still find me shrewish?"

"Not at all, though I wouldn't mind you ordering me about, especially in a moment like this."

She smiled mischievously as she ground her hips down. "Then allow me to do just that."

Overcome with a surge of love, John had to work to catch his breath. "I am the luckiest of men," he said roughly, his throat tight. "I love you beyond words."

"Good, because I don't want you to talk anymore." She moved her hips and reached between them to stroke his sex. "Instead, you can show me how much you love me, and as you take me to my release, I will shout my love for you to the rafters."

John grinned. "You'll get us expelled from the inn."

She arched a brow in response.

In the end, she did shout her love, and no one said a word.

～

December 1787

*I*t was not, in fact, a year before they conceived a child. Indeed, if one were counting, the babe came less than nine months following the wedding.

Angelica Cecilia Rowley entered the world squalling and red-faced. Cecilia and John could not have been happier.

Now that she was two and a half months old, Angelica still screamed from time to time, but generally, she smiled and laughed and completely delighted her parents.

"Your grandmamas and grandpapas will be here later," Cecilia cooed to her daughter as they lay on the floor together. Angelica was on her belly and trying valiantly to lift her head. "John, I think she may be trying to roll over."

"Nurse said she would likely do that soon," he said from where he sat nearby on the floor.

"Will I ever tire of watching her?" It wasn't a question that required an answer, for Cecilia already knew, and it was no. Never. Cecilia would be intent upon her daughter for the rest of her days.

"It's hard to imagine that we wanted to wait to have children," John said with a chuckle.

Cecilia looked over at him before patting Angelica's back. "I believe there was a time or two that you were just a hair too late in leaving me."

"Perhaps. But I did tell you that method isn't entirely reliable."

"Of course it isn't." When Cecilia had learned she was carrying, her first response had been fear. What if she wasn't a good mother? What if she didn't survive birthing the baby? Worse, what if the babe didn't survive?

Thankfully, none of those things had happened. Cecilia hoped she was a good mother. John certainly took every opportunity to tell her that she was.

Angelica grunted, and her face started to turn red. She was either emptying her bowels or growing frustrated.

Cecilia pushed herself up to sit on the floor. "All right, my darling girl?" she asked as she scooped Angelica into her arms and set the babe on her legs.

"I recognize that face. Time to ring for Nurse."

"John Rowley, you will not. Nurse is taking her respite, and I am quite capable of changing Lady Angelica's clout." Cecilia knew he was in jest. Still, she added, "And you will help."

He nodded solemnly. "Always. I am as smitten with our daughter as you are, even when she's filled her clout."

Angelica had settled when she arrived on Cecilia's lap. Cecilia leaned forward and sniffed. "I think she was just growing frustrated with being on her belly on the floor."

John scooted closer to them and stroked Angelica's wispy blonde hair. "Do you know what today is?" he asked Cecilia.

"The one-year anniversary of the day I meant to ensure you were stranded during the Yule Log Hunt."

"It's also the one-year anniversary of the day—and night—we had to shelter alone."

"The one-year anniversary of the day I stopped thinking of you as a menace."

"The one-year anniversary of the day I realized

you were never a shrew." John's lips met hers, and the resulting kiss made Cecilia melt.

"Too bad I have a baby on my lap," she murmured as he licked along her neck. "Nurse will be back soon."

"Not *that* soon," he said against her flesh.

"John, if you can't keep your hands, and other body parts, to yourself, there will soon be another baby."

He kissed his way up to her ear and whispered, "Would you mind?"

Cecilia shivered. "No. Blast, you're making my breasts tingle and my milk is starting to leak." She glanced down at Angelica to see if she'd noticed. The babe's head pitched forward towards Cecilia's chest. She was most definitely aware.

"Well, now I must feed your daughter," Cecilia said. "Take her so I can stand up."

John swept their daughter into his arms and held her against him with one while he helped Cecilia to stand with the other. Before he could hand Angelica back to Cecilia, there came the definitive sound of Angelica filling her clout. Angelica grunted again, then smiled.

Cecilia laughed. "Yes, you should be quite proud of yourself, darling girl."

"Come, my brilliant daughter," John said. "Let us adjourn to the nursery and see if you need a bath."

He started toward the door of the drawing room, and Cecilia followed. "I can take her if you like," she offered.

"I am going to change Angelica's clout, and you can't stop me."

Cecilia's heart swelled. This man had exceeded every one of her expectations as well as her dreams. He was kind, helpful, devoted, and in possession of a wickedly passionate nature that simply made being with him joyful.

She trailed him to the nursery, which currently adjoined their bedchamber so that Cecilia could be close to Angelica for feeding. Then she watched as he peeled away Angelica's clothing and tidied her with a care and thoroughness that would have shocked anyone—except Cecilia. She knew what a wonderful man she'd married.

"If you could convince the other men of your station to do that, you'd be the most beloved man in England."

He snorted. "Not by those men. They'd hate me."

"Not if you persuaded them so that they were eager to help." Cecilia had no doubt he could do it. The man was born to speak, and she knew he'd be an excellent addition to the House of Commons when there was next an opportunity for him to stand.

"I am working on Spetch."

"So Dinah told me in her last letter." They had welcomed a son in the summer.

John cradled Angelica as he turned toward Cecilia. "All clean and ready for her meal, my lady."

"Thank you, my lord." Cecilia sat down in her favorite chair near the hearth and unfastened her round gown to feed her hungry daughter. A short while later, Angelica had fallen asleep. John came to take her once more and settled her into her bassinet.

Cecilia had refastened her garments, and now John pulled her gently to her feet. "Do you require a nap as well?" he asked.

"I think I'd like a respite in our bed," She gave him a suggestive look.

"What about Nurse? Will she be back soon?"

"Not for another thirty minutes or so. But she doesn't need to be here. We'll leave the door partially open so we can hear Angelica if she needs us."

He looked at her with open admiration. "You're so confident, as if you were meant to be a mother."

"I'm not sure I always feel confident, but I do love being a mother. As much as I adore being your wife. Now, hurry along so I can show you that adoration." She walked past him into their bedchamber.

"I love it when you command me." He came up behind her and wrapped his arms around her middle.

She arched her neck in invitation, and he instantly latched his lips onto her flesh. "And I love it when you obey."

~

January 1802

*I*n the late morning of John and Cecilia's fifteenth wedding anniversary, John sat in his study reading correspondence. The sound of running feet and shouts thundered from the stair hall, and he wondered what mischief his children were up to. There were five of them, ranging from Angelica who was fourteen, to Cecily who was six. In between were Brom, the twelve-year old heir, Felix, the ten-year old spare, and eight-year-old Susan, who'd been named for Cecilia's dear great-aunt who'd unfortunately died three years earlier.

Cecilia suddenly dashed into the study and closed the door. She put her finger to her lips. Her eyes danced with mirth.

"Playing hide-and-seek again?" John asked. "Aren't you supposed to stay hidden in the same place?"

"I was crouched under a table in the library, and my legs began to ache. And I was growing bored. Now, you can entertain me."

John laughed, and she immediately waved her hand to quiet him. "Shhh!"

He stood from behind his desk and went to join her where she stood behind the door. "Is this your hiding spot?" he whispered, pulling her to his chest.

"I was just going to hide behind the door if they came in."

"If? You don't think they'll look here?"

"They won't wish to bother you since the door is closed."

"So you've made it so they can't possibly find you. That hardly seems fair." He nuzzled her neck, inhaling her scent. He would never tire of the way she smelled or how she felt in his arms.

"Blast, I didn't mean to. Would you mind cracking the door open, then?"

John kissed the spot beneath her ear. "I'm inclined to leave it closed. You know what today is, don't you?"

"Of course I do. I know that you are taking me somewhere mysterious this afternoon." She glanced toward his desk. "Unless you're too busy?"

"I'm never too busy to spend time with my bride, especially on the day we were wed." John had been serving in the House of Commons twelve years now, but his family was his priority.

"Aren't you going to open the door?" she asked.

Reluctantly, John left her side and opened the door halfway. They were immediately besieged by their brood. Except Angelica. She was likely with her French tutor.

"Found you!" Brom, which was short for Bromwell, as they'd named him after Cecilia's family, exclaimed. John's heart squeezed, for Brom would go off to Eton this year, and the house would grow infinitely quieter.

The children rushed at Cecilia, who laughed with glee. "At last," she said. "I had to move from my original spot because I was bored."

"You're the best hider, Mama," Cecily said as she clung to Cecilia's skirts.

"Come, we've all earned a treat. Let's see what Cook has for us." Cecilia ushered them toward the door. She looked back over her shoulder at John with an expectant smile. "I'll see you later."

John could hardly wait.

Later that day

*C*ecilia snuggled next to John as they ambled along a track that edged the estate. "Why are we not in a coach? Or at least on horseback?"

"Because I didn't want a coachman or horses. It's our anniversary, and I wanted some time alone with my wife." He glanced down at her. "That is not always easy to secure."

"True." With their five children, Cecilia's duties managing their households, and John's responsibilities in Parliament, they led very busy lives. "I am cold, though."

"Not for long," he promised.

Cecilia had no idea what he had in store, but

was eager to find out. "I've an idea for the house party this autumn," she said to focus on something other than feeling cold.

"Something new?"

They'd hosted a house party every autumn starting the year after Angelica was born. Except for the year Felix was born, because he'd also arrived in September. The other children had come in the spring.

"You know my family is known for making matches."

"I do."

"Well, I have yet to facilitate one." And Cecilia's mother reminded her often.

"You will when Angelica is of age, I'm certain."

"I hope so. However, I'd like to try to make a match at the house party. I'm looking for an eligible bachelor or a young lady ready for marriage who perhaps doesn't wish to participate in the Season."

"Do such young ladies exist?"

Cecilia knew he was joking. "Certainly. London can be quite intimidating. If I can help a young lady who would prefer to avoid that, would I not be providing a kindness?"

"Indeed you would. But then you are the soul of kindness, my love. Ah, here we are." John guided her from the track into a copse of trees.

"Oh no, you're taking me into the forest so I'll get lost, aren't you? Have you been planning your revenge for fifteen years?"

John laughed. "Hardly. Though I have been planning this awhile." They stepped from the trees, and a small cottage came into view. Smoke curled from the chimney.

Cecilia gasped. "It looks just like our cottage! I mean, the woodcutter's cottage at Broadheath."

"It is an exact replica," John said. "Though the interior is slightly changed."

She rushed forward and threw open the door. "*Slightly?*"

The space was still small, but there was a larger bed situated before the fire as well as a table with two chairs. There were also cupboards and a wash-basin. And an armoire. Curious, she went to the latter and opened the doors. Inside, there were nightclothes and blankets as well as extra shoes and cloaks. "Is this in case we become stranded?" she asked.

John smiled, his eyes glowing. "If we're so lucky."

"I am already the luckiest," Cecilia whispered as she moved into his arms. He kissed her, and it was like the first time. The same magic swept over her, transporting her to that day over fifteen years ago when their lives had changed.

She pulled her lips from his and looked into his eyes. "This is perhaps the least impulsive thing you've ever done. How long did it take you to plan and execute this? I had no idea."

"Over a year ago. I had to find the right spot and then have it built."

"You've decorated it beautifully." She stepped from his arms and went to run her hand over the velvet coverlet on the bed. "It's so cozy and lush. I may never want to leave."

"That may have been my intent." He prowled toward her with dark promise glittering in his gaze.

A movement in the window behind him caught her eye. Snowflakes were fluttering past and onto the panes. "It's snowing!" She strode past him to peer outside.

He joined her, smiling. "That was not my plan, but I certainly hoped for it."

Cecilia turned toward him. "I do hope those cupboards contain food."

"They do, but all I need to get through this day, and this life, is you."

She curled her arms around his neck. "I do love you, my menace."

He lowered his head toward hers. "And I love you, shrew."

Catch up with Cecilia and John in THE RIGID DUKE (if you haven't already), book two of the *Matchmaking Chronicles*! Cecilia hosts a party to help match the Duke of Warrington, whose surly nature has prohibited him from finding a duchess—not that he particularly wants one. But when the seemingly perfect bride is thrust before him, he is instead drawn to her refinement tutor, a frustratingly sunny and buoyant widow who has him rethinking his wife choices.

Read on for chapter one of *THE RIGID DUKE*!

THE RIGID DUKE
CHAPTER ONE

September 1802

"Marina has made a great deal of progress this summer." Mrs. Juno Langton smiled brightly at her employer, Lady Wetherby. "I daresay she could attempt a short stint in York this fall."

With a wide, furrowed brow and pursed lips, Lady Wetherby didn't appear convinced. But why should she? Her daughter, Marina, was a social disaster. *Was.* Juno's job was to fix that, and she *had* made some progress. However, perhaps describing it as "a great deal" was a slight exaggeration.

"In what specific ways has she improved?" the countess asked from the opposite chair in her private sitting room, where they met weekly to discuss Marina.

"Her dancing." Because they practiced over an hour every day. "Her ease at conversation." Also because they practiced over an hour every day. And Juno wasn't shortsighted about it—she knew Marina's comfort had increased with *her*, but would take some finessing once they got to London. Or York, which would be an excellent rehearsal for London.

"What about smiling?" Lady Wetherby asked. "I haven't seen her smile any more than she did before. Which was hardly at all." She gave her head a tiny shake.

"That is also improving." Again, Juno had found success with Marina, but couldn't be certain her charge would smile with other people. At least not at first. That was the problem. Until Marina got to know someone, she was completely uncomfortable in their presence. She didn't make eye contact, she fidgeted, and she barely said a word. Juno could well imagine how it was that no gentleman danced with her a second time—not at a single ball but during the *entire* Season.

"I'm not seeing it, but then I think Marina takes pleasure in behaving in an especially surly manner with me." Lady Wetherby's lips pursed even more. Juno wondered if they might shrivel up and disappear.

"I don't believe that's true, my lady," Juno said with a reassuring smile. "I think, with respect, that Marina wants to please you and knows she hasn't."

Lady Wetherby's nostrils flared. "Are you saying it's my fault she's cold and awkward?"

"Not at all." Though she wasn't terribly wrong… "Perhaps if you gave her more encouragement, you might be rewarded with her demonstrating the progress she's made." Juno offered her widest smile, which typically thawed even the most frigid people. Not that Lady Wetherby was frigid. Well, perhaps she was when it came to her eldest child. Juno had seen the countess with her younger children, and she seemed far more relaxed.

"I'll do that," Lady Wetherby said before exhaling a rather beleaguered sigh. "I'm sure you're right that she is making progress. That is the reason we hired you after departing London early."

Juno had finished her prior contract of employment sooner than she'd planned when her former charge had snared an earl. The family had been overjoyed with Juno's tutelage, and Juno had been thrilled to take some time for herself, adjourning to Bath, where she'd spent a lovely fortnight in the strong arms of a charming captain. It might have been longer except she'd received the offer from the Wetherbys to attend their daughter, who was in dire need of refinement after a disastrous first Season. Unable to resist the challenge—or the pay—Juno had left her captain and traveled north to Yorkshire.

"I do fear she is destined for spinsterhood," Lady Wetherby said with a frown, drawing Juno back to the present.

"I am confident we can avoid that. The right husband is out there for Marina. We just have to find him. I do think a short stint to York may be just the thing." Juno wanted Marina to be able to practice her newfound skills in social settings outside the bustle and pressure of the Season.

"I agree," Lady Wetherby said, clasping her hands in her lap. "Not about York, but that the right husband is out there. To that end, we've been invited to a house party next month. The Duke of Warrington will be in attendance. He is rumored to detest the Marriage Mart, but is also in need of a wife. It's the perfect opportunity to secure a match between him and Marina." Her blue eyes positively glowed with anticipation and confidence. As if the betrothal between Marina and the duke were a *fait accompli*.

Juno was only vaguely aware of the duke. He did not seem to be a social sort, which made it easy to believe that he didn't care for the Marriage

Mart. Matching someone like him with someone like Marina would be…challenging.

Juno absolutely loved a challenge. That was how she'd embarked on this career of helping young ladies bring their natural confidence and charm to the fore following the death of her husband. Dashing Bernard Langton had swept a naïve young Juno into a mad love affair and marriage, shocking her parents and prompting them to disassociate from their only daughter.

After less than a year, Bernard had died, leaving Juno without family or funds. She'd leapt at the chance to be companion to an elderly lady. When she'd helped that lady's granddaughter secure an upwardly mobile marriage, Juno's career as a companion, or more accurately "refinement tutor," had been born.

"Shall I summon Marina to join us?" Juno suggested, hoping her charge would be up to the task of gaining her mother's approval. That was, unfortunately, no small feat.

"I asked Dale to send her in after a while." Lady Wetherby directed her gaze to the doorway, which was behind Juno. "Here she is."

Juno turned her head to see Marina walk cautiously into the sitting room. Dressed in a simple pale blue day gown, Marina fidgeted with her fingers as she approached, her blue eyes downcast.

"Look up, dear," Lady Wetherby said with a bit of snap to her tone.

"Come and join us, Marina." Juno stood and moved to a settee so Marina could sit beside her.

Marina's gaze lifted to briefly meet Juno's before she moved to the settee. Once seated, she plucked at the skirt of her gown.

"Do stop that." Lady Wetherby frowned at her daughter.

Juno edged closer to Marina, hoping her presence would be a comforting influence. "We have exciting news to share."

Marina glanced toward her as her fingers stilled. Straightening, she sat as Juno had taught her—shoulders back, spine stiff, chin up, slight smile in place. Pride shot through Juno, as well as glee that Marina had found the courage to do what she must in her mother's presence.

Lady Wetherby's features flashed with surprise and perhaps a dash of approval. "We are to attend a house party next month. The Duke of Warrington will be in attendance, and he is in search of a wife. My darling, you could snag a duke without having to suffer another Season."

Juno felt a burst of tenderness at the warmth in the countess's tone. She might be frustrated by her daughter—and certainly didn't understand her—but she wanted the best for her, including the chance to avoid a Season, which she knew Marina had loathed.

Instead of responding with relief at this prospect, Marina crumpled, her face falling into a deep scowl. "Must I, Mother?"

"I'm afraid so." The countess had stiffened, her face freezing in disappointment. "I do hope you can summon the appropriate enthusiasm."

Turning toward her charge, Juno gently touched the young woman's arm. "Just think, you'll have a chance to practice everything we've worked on. A house party is the perfect place to gain confidence and hone your skills."

"I barely have any of either," Marina said quietly, shooting a perturbed look toward her mother. "But I suppose I have no choice."

"That is correct," Lady Wetherby said firmly. "We leave in a fortnight." Her expression gentled once more. "The duke doesn't care for the Marriage Mart either. Perhaps the two of you will find an accord. I think this could be just the match you've been waiting for."

"I haven't been waiting for any match," Marina muttered. "May I go now?"

"Yes." The countess looked rather despondent as her daughter stood and shuffled from the room.

Juno tensed as she readjusted herself on the settee to face her employer. "She'll be ready for the house party. She just needs to acclimate herself. We've plenty of time to prepare."

"I hope you're right, considering what I'm paying you. In fact, if you can ensure this betrothal occurs, I'll increase your pay twenty percent." Lady Wetherby stood. "Do not let us down, Mrs. Langton."

The countess swept from the room, and Juno narrowed her eyes in contemplation. A fortnight to not only ensure Marina was ready for a house party, but that she could snare a duke. It would be Juno's most daunting challenge yet.

She leapt to her feet, eager to get started.

Alexander Brett, Duke of Warrington, stalked into the drawing room at precisely a quarter of an hour before six. His mother, seated serenely on the dark red settee, came from the dower house most evenings to dine with him.

She surveyed him as he went to pour a glass of her favorite madeira and a brandy for himself. "How was your day?"

After handing her the wine, he sat in the chair near her settee. Same drinks, same seating arrangement, same question to begin their conversation. He liked same.

"Productive."

"As always," she murmured. "I don't suppose anything exciting happened?"

"The post was greater than usual." He sipped his brandy.

"Anything of interest?"

"Not to me, though you would probably find the invitation to a house party notable."

His mother, in her early fifties with still-dark hair, save a few strands of gray at her temples, sat a bit taller. "What house party? When?" Her sable eyes sparked with enthusiasm.

"Doesn't matter. I'm not going."

She pursed her lips at him before relaxing. He could see she was choosing her words, lining up her soldiers for the coming battle. "But you should. I realize you don't care for social situations; however, this is a small gathering, not at all like the events of the Season."

Dare, the name he'd been called his entire life, which was a shortened version of the courtesy title he'd held—Marquess of Daresbury—before his father's death three years earlier, narrowed his eyes at his mother. "You're behind this invitation."

"What makes you think that?" She tried to sound innocent, but her gaze darted to the side and her voice rose. When he said nothing, she looked back to him and exhaled. "Fine. Yes."

"Am I to understand you convinced Lady Cosford to host a house party so that I might attend?"

"Of course not. I merely made a few well-placed comments to friends in recent months."

"What sort of comments?"

"That you are in search of a wife." She gave him

an exasperated look. "Well, you *are*." Frowning at him, she took an irritated sip of madeira.

"And that somehow led to an invitation to a house party that I have no desire to attend." He made a sound low in his throat before taking another drink of brandy.

"Don't growl. It's so off-putting."

"I don't growl."

His mother arched a thick, dark brow, then shook her head, apparently deciding that was a battle she didn't care to wage. "You should accept the invitation. You do need a wife, and I should think finding one at a small house party in Warwickshire would be far more appealing than attempting the Marriage Mart in London come spring."

Dare shuddered. He couldn't think of anything he'd rather do less. His mother was, unfortunately, correct. He did need a wife. Furthermore, he'd been lamenting how he might find one given that he hated, as his mother had put it, social situations.

What if there wasn't anyone at the house party he would consider marrying? He scrutinized his mother and gave her the credit she was due. "What is the young lady's name?"

She looked at him in surprise, as if he couldn't guess she was scheming a particular match. Faint pink brightened her cheeks, but the color was fleeting. "Lady Marina Fellowes, eldest daughter of the Earl of Wetherby. I'm sure you know him."

They worked together in the House of Lords. Wetherby didn't care for idle chatter and always got right to the heart of things. Dare hadn't even realized he had a daughter. Or a family, for that matter. Perhaps his daughter wouldn't be the typical prattle basket that most young ladies were.

"What's she like?" he asked cautiously.

The vigor with which his mother answered almost made him sorry he'd expressed even the slightest interest. "Very pretty and quite accomplished at needlework."

"That tells me nothing. Is she a featherbrain or not?"

"I doubt it."

That was not a promising answer. Perhaps his mother didn't know her. "Has she even had a Season?"

"Yes, just this past one." His mother's features brightened. "You should like this bit. She returned to the country early. I'm not sure London—rather, the social whirl—is to her liking."

"You should have started with that," Dare muttered. If Lady Marina was cut from the same cloth as her father—and why wouldn't she be?—this house party actually had potential. "I'll go to the party to meet Lady Marina."

"To see if you will suit?"

Dare glowered at his mother's obvious glee. "Yes."

She laughed. "You always try so hard to be brusque, even when presented with an opportunity that could help you achieve your aims without suffering that which you find utterly bothersome."

Loathsome was a better word. Shopping for a wife made him itch.

Some of his mother's enthusiasm dimmed. "Should I come with you? I think I sh—"

"*No.*" He didn't let her finish. If she accompanied him, he'd go mad under her attempts to see him betrothed.

She glared at him, but only for a moment. "So dour," she murmured. "Can you at least try to be charming? Perhaps smile a little?"

Smiling was for insincere people. When Dare

smiled, he meant it. "Why pretend to be someone I'm not? My future wife should know precisely whom she's marrying."

His mother exhaled. "That's what I'm afraid of." She paused, rallying her troops once more before she entered the breach. "If you can't be charming, you'll need to be...something. You can't expect to win Lady Marina's hand if you don't engage her somehow."

"I suppose I'll have to dance with her." He detested dancing.

"You could promenade. I'm sure there will be plenty of activities. Perhaps you can go for a ride together."

"That would be acceptable." He would appreciate a wife who enjoyed riding. He imagined her touring the estate with him, speaking to the tenants, and offering assistance and support.

"I'm relieved to hear it."

He shrugged. "Although, being a duke is likely enough to win the chit's—or anyone else's—hand."

His mother stared at him, then took a long drink of madeira, nearly draining the glass. "If that's what you think, you deserve a wife who only wants you for your title."

It seemed the battle this evening would go to his mother.

"I am more than my title," he said quietly, and not without a hint of irritation.

"Of course you are, and I hope you realize it. I also hope you find the woman who breaks through that rigid outer shell you wield so relentlessly. She won't see your title at all, and she'll warm to you, in spite of your efforts to keep her away."

Dare blinked. "I won't do that."

"That's all you do, my darling," she said with a loving glow that slightly melted his hardened exterior. He did keep up a wall, and he liked it. Inside his fortress, things were orderly and expected. He hated mess and emotion and anything surprising. The woman for him would understand that and leave him be.

Perhaps his mother was right—he would hold his duchess apart. Was that so bad? "You are far too sentimental, Mother."

The butler entered and announced that dinner was served. Dare finished his brandy, and his mother did the same with her madeira. After depositing their empty glasses on a table for the butler to sweep away, Dare helped the dowager to her feet and offered his arm.

She placed her hand on his sleeve, and they walked into the dining room as they did every night. Peace settled over him. *Same.*

"I love you, my boy," she whispered just before taking her chair.

That was different. Dare was surprised that he didn't mind.